Streakers

Streakers

Gary Davison

Paperbooks Ltd, 3rd Floor, Unicorn House
London E1 6PJ
info@legend-paperbooks.co.uk
www.paperbooks.co.uk

British Library Cataloguing in Publication Data available.

ISBN 978-1-9065585-2-9

Set in Times
Printed by J F Print Ltd., Sparkford, Somerset.

Cover designed by:
Gudrun Jobst
www.yotedesign.com

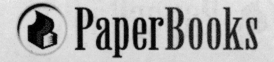

For Michael McCormack

Also by Gary Davison

Fat Tuesday

see www.paperbooks.co.uk for details

Acknowledgements

Karen Davison
Tom Chalmers
Lorna Read
Pauline Davison
Lindsey Thornton
Harvey Thornton

Oscar fans recently voted Robert Opel's streak past David Niven in 1974 as the top Oscar moment, beating John Wayne's final public appearance to the award.

1

I've worked in the Fiddler's Arms in Faccome By The Sea town centre for about two years. Since I dropped out of uni. It's a smoky old hole on the high street, popular with daytime drinkers and weekend stag parties warming up to head into Newcastle. On a normal Saturday afternoon there would be nothing I couldn't handle on my own, but today Faccome FC were playing Darlington in the first round proper of the FA cup.

It was a late morning kick-off and straight after the match we were heaving. I swear I've seen nothing like it in here before. It was six deep at the bar, and all they were talking and singing about was the masked streaker. The Faccome Flash. Men reasoned that had he not come on when he did, we'd never have got the equaliser: shook the whole game up... didn't know what had hit 'em, he's the real star, has to be some sort of athlete...

The women were in a worse state over this streaker than the men. They seemed to be drunk before they even got through the doors, falling all over each other, hanging on to anybody they could. Women as old as my mother, saying how they would do this to him and give him good that: twelve on the slack at least... banging round his knees... can't be local or I'd have had some of that by now. Husbands and boyfriends were being harshly eliminated as suspects.

A couple more part-timers had arrived and I took a breather. I stood at the side of the bar, next to the poolroom door. I opened a can of Diet Coke and eavesdropped on a conversation between a group of girls, mid-twenties, all covered in fake tan, their white jacket elbows scruffy and soaking from leaning on the bar.

'There's nothing,' one slurred, 'and I mean *nothing*, I wouldn't do for a man built like that.'

'Me neither. Would you go twos up?'

'Would you?'

'Fucking right I would!'

They flung their orange faces back laughing.

Sam, my flatmate, arrived to start his shift. Sam's six foot one and has cropped blond hair and starey blue eyes. My mother says he looks Icelandic (because she saw a film starring Sam's double, wearing a white fur coat and riding a sledge pulled by huskies). Sam looks more like a tennis player coming into his prime, a leaner, cockier, Boris Becker in his Wimbledon heyday.

'Christ, it's manic in here,' he said, ditching his jacket. 'Did you hear about the streaker?'

'Like anything else has happened today.'

The men had now congregated away from the

women, forming a united front against accusations of having a tiddler. No matter what the men came back with, though, the women always finished with the upper hand, chanting, 'Off! Off! Off!'

The first woman up on a table with her tits out wasn't too bad at all. Unfortunately, the fatties saw this as an opportunity to impress and took to the tables in numbers, juggling them about with their hands and threatening to remove their skirts. With the new temporary manager nowhere in sight, Sam and I went round and guided them back down onto the floor. No sooner had one topless beauty been helped down then another got up, trying to outdo the last. The women at ground level were tearing at our clothes and groping us between the legs, while the men pelted us with sausage rolls for spoiling their fun. After unclamping a woman from Sam's back, we took refuge behind the bar.

By ten o'clock, everyone was in such a state that we decided not to call last orders and started steering the zombies out the door. It took over an hour to get them out and keep them out.

Sam joined me in a booth at the front window with a couple of pints and we lit up.

The place was wrecked.

We had probably taken in one night what we normally take in a week. More.

Sam lifted a black bra off the floor with his foot. 'If you hadn't witnesses the show, finding the owner of this would be top of the agenda.'

'How white were her tits?'

'How veiny?'

'The first one was the best, I was all for slipping into her after last orders, but…'

'But what? When was the last time you done the deed?'

'I get by.'

'How long?'

'Not that long.'

'Month?'

A lonely whistle interrupted the inevitable onslaught from Sam about my recent drought.

The whistle got louder as the person came along the passage. I tried to place the tune – *and you want my body come on sugar let me know…*

Brian, the temporary manager, appeared behind the bar and went straight for the optics and poured himself a whisky. Brian's about five-six, mid-to-late fifties, and has jet-black curly hair that hangs over his ears like a hunting hat. He was wearing black pants and a black waistcoat over a wrinkled white shirt. He's really stooped over and after introducing himself this morning, I'd only caught glimpses of him wiping the odd table and talking to the old timers in the corner.

Brian came from behind the bar, shuffling along with his whisky, totally oblivious to us. 'Brian.'

His hands shot up to his face and his drink went flying over his shoulder.

Sam and I stifled a laugh.

Brian picked up his empty glass, then came over.

'Brian, this is Sam, another part-timer.'

Brian stuck out a shaky hand. 'Please to meet you, Sam.'

Sam stood up, towering over Brian, who clumsily stepped back out the way. 'And you. Bit of a baptism for you tonight, Brian, eh?'

'Yes. Is it always this busy?'

Sam walked off without answering and started hoovering.

Brian and I had a smoke and a Jack Daniels and talked about the match. I asked him how long he had worked in bars and he said, on and off, about ten years. This was his first job in over a year, though. Without any prompting he changed the subject and told me about his daughter, who worked as a nurse in South Africa. How her husband – soon to be ex-husband – was a bully, and that if his back hadn't been so bad, he'd have given the bastard a good hiding. Brian said that his daughter wanted him to go and live with her, once the divorce was through and things had settled down. She could find him a job, a good job, well paid, no sweat.

Sam was on my case to get back and watch *Match of the Day* and his blatant huffing and puffing as he passed us was making Brian uneasy.

I got up and emptied the drip trays and recorded the waste, then filled the glass washer and mopped the bar floor. Brian emptied ashtrays and collected glasses. Sam finished hoovering then speed-cleaned the tables, before joining me behind the bar.

'You have taped it, haven't you?' he asked me again.

'Are you for real? How many times do I have to tell you?'

I switched the fridge lights off and went over to Brian, who was having a smoke and another whisky. 'That's us done, Brian. You just need to cash up. The rota's on the wall in your office for the rest of the week.'

'Thanks. Thanks for helping me settle in. It's been a while since I've been behind a bar.'

Sam was nudging me in the back. 'No probs. I'll see you Monday.'

Halfway along the passage, Brian shouted us back.

'What's up?' I asked.

He was standing in front of the till, petrified. 'It's one of those new ones. You couldn't cash up for me and I'll do tomorrow's, could you?'

'Yeah, no bother.'

Sam hissed in my ear: 'What if it hasn't taped? We'll miss it!'

I ignored him and printed the reports off.

Brian watched me, all sheepish at being such an inconvenience.

I finished cashing up and we headed home.

Our flat's on the tenth floor of a fourteen storey grey monstrosity a mile-and-half from the town centre.

Reaching the top of the bank, Sam took hold of my elbow again.

I stopped dead and pushed him away. 'Naff off.'

He looked at me, all confused.

'Don't give me that, you know what's up,' I said. 'That poor bloke hasn't got a clue and you're bouncing around trying to get out the door.'

'Al, please,' he said, walking towards me, arms open. 'I'm sorry. I'm just excited to see the match. I'll make him double welcome tomorrow. Honest. Now let's get back and watch the match of the decade.'

I reluctantly followed him, brushing his hand away as he tried to steer me through the doors.

We got in the flat and plonked down opposite each other on our sofas with a beer and started the tape.

Darlington took the lead early with a deflected free kick. Coverage soon skipped to the second half and Darlington continued bombarding our goal. We were being completely outclassed and if I didn't already know the result, I would have been praying for the final whistle. Instead, I was scouring the touchlines for the streaker.

'Any second, Al. Keep watching their goal. Come on!'

With less than ten minutes to go, the masked streaker burst onto the pitch from behind the away goal. Sam and I were screaming and hugging each other as he tore across the pitch, swerving past players like they were statues. The Faccome Flash reached our goal, turned on his heels and saluted the crowd, before bolting for the corner of the ground and making his escape over the concrete wall.

Sam and I remained standing, arm over each other's shoulders, cheering Faccome on as they went right at Darlington. The referee was struggling to keep control and minutes later awarded us a free kick wide right in the Darlington half. Everyone was forward, jostling for space on the edge of the eighteen-yard box. Peter Healy launched the ball in. It was headed out and time stood still as Stevey Earnshaw, the youngest player out there, kept his eye on the ball, watched it down, then unleashed a-once-in-a-lifetime volley into the top corner.

What a goal! What a goal!

Sam and I were jumping all over, sprinting into the kitchen and back impersonating the streaker. It was all down to him! He changed everything!

By the time we calmed down, another match was playing.

Sam fetched some more beers and I rewound the video.

I sat crossed-legged in front of the TV and pressed play. The moment he came into sight the crowd went berserk. The obvious had been blanked out for the television but as they showed a close-up of him, turning to salute the crowd, something caught my eye.

I rewound it and froze it on the close-up. The streaker was wearing a black mask, dark socks and white trainers. The freeze frame wasn't the best, so I re-ran it again, keeping my eye on his socks. I glanced at Sam – knees to chest rocking on the sofa – then back at the Jesmond Tennis Club socks the streaker was wearing. The same socks I had borrowed from my mother's a few weeks ago.

I yanked Sam's trouser leg up. 'It's you, isn't it?'

2

Sam sprang off the sofa and into his room.

I stood at the front window watching a lad trying to flag a taxi down in the rain, waiting for Sam to come out and deny it; to put me straight and tell me he'd just put the socks on when he came in, or that he hadn't made it to the match after all.

His bedroom door creaked open.

I slowly turned around, and casually leaning against the doorframe in a black leather mask and black underpants was The Faccome Flash.

It might as well have been a Bengal tiger standing there, I was so stunned.

Sam went into the kitchen and came back out with a bottle of vodka from his stash and walked towards me.

We circled each other like two bare-knuckle fighters, before settling down on our sofas.

I swear I could hardly look at him, let alone say anything. I've known him since we were four years old. And here he was, sitting opposite me in a gimp mask after streaking in front of millions. If I'd found that mask in his room, I would have been asking questions, but this? This was... what was this, for Christ's sakes?

I looked over at him and I knew he was smiling under the mask and loving every second of this. My mind was jumping from the football pitch to him standing at the bedroom door and there was nothing in between. My flat mate was quite simply off his head. He now thought it was normal to run naked, without any warning, in front of the nation. What the hell was he thinking of?

Sam pulled the mask off and threw it over, along with the bottle of vodka.

I took a swig of vodka, then held the mask out in front of me, running my finger along the mouth zip. 'Where did you get this from?'

'Sex shop on Grainger Street.'

'Hold on, hold on,' I said, getting up. 'Let me get this right. You woke up this morning and decided to go into Newcastle to buy a gimp mask so you could run bollicky in front of the whole town?'

'I was already going to the sex shop for something else, I just saw that and, well, you know, honestly, Al, your face.'

'My face! My face! What the fuck do you expect, you lunatic?'

Sam snatched the mask, pulled it on, and took off round the flat, screaming.

I had another swig of vodka.

I needed to get pissed quick.

Sam ended his lap of honour with a swan dive onto his sofa.

We both calmed down, passing the bottle between us.

Sam told me that he had decided to do it this morning after reading about a streaker in FHM. He hadn't expected anything like the reaction we had witnessed in The Fiddler's, though. 'I just thought it would be a frisk and me and you'd have a laugh watching it tonight.'

The vodka was kicking in and I was starting to make some sense of it, now that I knew why he'd ended up doing it. Sam's always been a bit off-the-wall – never to this extent before, but he's had me on my toes loads of times. I remember once in The Fiddlers. It was a Saturday night and the place was half empty. A lad, about the same age as us, was standing at the corner of the bar with his girlfriend. She was gorgeous, and we were keeping tabs on her behind the boyfriend's back. Just as the jukebox stopped playing, the boyfriend moved about three yards away to the cigarette machine. Sam leant over the bar, turned the girl's face towards him and started kissing her. With a second to spare they broke off. The moment was so tense, I'll never forget it. Later, Sam shrugged it off like it was nothing. I spent the night replaying the scene in my mind, him kissing her, the boyfriend putting his money in the cigarette machine, each coin dropping down, the seconds ticking away. To anyone watching, it was surreal, a situation that could blow up into violence any second. To Sam, it was just a laugh.

I tried the mask on. 'I can hardly hear anything,' I said, shaking my head.

'Honestly, Al, when I ran out it was deafening. I felt so fast and powerful I could have run round the pitch all day and they'd never have caught me.'

I took the mask off and we watched Match of the Day again.

We kept glancing over at each other and laughing.

Every so often I tweaked between my legs, feeling totally inadequate.

I fell asleep clutching the mask and vodka bottle.

*

I woke up in the morning in the same position. The phone was ringing.

I stumbled into my bedroom and reached for my dream journal. The crowd was going crazy as I sprinted into the centre circle, arm aloft. As the stewards closed in from both sides, I ran down the centre and veered off towards the corner exit. The tunnel was blocked. I turned back up the touchline and the steward closest to me was Sam. I stopped and looked around – all the stewards and players were Sam. I backed away, edging into the crowd – they were all Sam, too.

I flopped back onto my bed and massaged my eyes.

I got into this dream analysis stuff about six months ago after watching a television programme about it. At first, I just looked up a few things that were in the dream and tried to suss out what my subconscious was trying to tell me. I did this a couple of times a week, usually after a weekend when I didn't have much on. When something easily identifiable was in my dream, like a person I knew, analysing the dream helped me work out what I really thought of a situation, or what my true feelings were for that person. Often things that had been on my mind for ages, not necessarily problems, I felt comfortable with and stopped thinking about them so much.

I also became fascinated with other people's dreams and I got punters in the bar to tell me about theirs. One regular, who was having marital problems, said he had had a reccurring dream for years, about flying high off buildings and swooping through the town centre at night. He had seen a counsellor with his wife while they were trying to work things out and the counsellor had said it was connected to him owning his own business and the power he had. I looked up flying dreams and they can also indicate sexual potency and a temptation to women.

That's the great thing about dreamwork, there's no right or wrong answer. Dreams tell you the truth about who you are, though, and the more honest you are, the more accurate the result. I'm right into it now and use everything I can remember to get the best analysis.

Last night's dream was so important because it was number fifty in a sequence I've been recording. This is the number they recommend you analyse to get an accurate picture of your entire psyche. Only problem is, last night's dream had hardly any of the reccurring elements of the regular dreams. Hopefully, it'll be a one-off, or all I'll know about myself will be next to nothing.

The phone rang again.

I went into the living room and answered it.

'Alex?'

I didn't recognise the voice. 'Yeah, who's that?'

'It's Brian. At the pub. I'm sorry to disturb you, but I need your help.'

Two part-timers hadn't showed up yet and there was already a queue outside.

I agreed to go in and bring Sam with me.

I made a coffee and opened the living room blinds.

It was overcast and drizzling.

I lay down on the sofa, wishing I hadn't agreed to go into work.

*

'Check the back pages out.' Sam was standing over me, in his running shorts and vest, dripping wet. 'News of the World and Mirror.'

I sat forward feeling worse than when I first woke up.

The Sunday Mirror was offering a £500 reward for Sam's identity, while the News of the World had dedicated the whole back page to him and had some blurred photos, probably taken with someone's mobile. The combination of being hung over and having Sam in my face had my head spinning. I gave him the good news about work and went to get dressed.

We headed down the bank towards town, Sam in a

denim jacket and woolly beanie, me in my green parka with the hood up. The trees were nearly all bare now and I couldn't help wishing that summer was on its way, rather than leaving. Hands in pockets, we jogged the last half-mile.

We came in the side entrance, took our jackets off and went into the bar.

It was 1 p.m. and the same crowd as yesterday were in, singing and chanting for The Faccome Flash, who had become an even bigger hero overnight because he had put Faccome on the back pages of all the nationals: increasing TV revenue for the return leg... tourism'll be up next summer... he'll come to the rescue again, no doubt.

There were four of us flat out, plus Brian, who was wandering around with his dishcloth.

Sam caught my attention and we nipped out back.

'Can you believe this?' he was saying, pacing around.

'Unreal. You could have any female in there, married or not.'

Sam wasn't listening. 'Yeah, yeah, look Al, I'm going to do it again.'

'They'll be watching for you next time, Sam, think about it.'

'If we plan my escape properly, I could get away. Imagine'

The whole town had gone stir crazy in a little over twenty-four hours because he had ran across a football pitch in the buff. The papers were offering cash rewards for his identity. If Sam pulled it off again, he would be so famous it would be untrue.

I snatched a cigarette out of my box and lit up. 'Every time you escaped, the bigger you'd become. A myth. A legend.'

'It's got to be the return leg at Darlington on Wednesday.'

'Tricky,' I said, exhaling. 'Their ground is built for the premiership. Security'll be tight. I'll tell you what, though, if you did, they'd make a film out of it. Imagine!'

'Imagine!'

We jumped up and down, hugging each other. We were going to be famous, loaded, women falling at our feet, TV interviews, film premieres, book deals, guest appearances...

The bar suddenly went quiet.

We walked along the passage and out into the bar.

The front door was wedged open with a wheelchair. The person sitting in it with their hood up was getting soaked with rain. Talking resumed at a low level. Sam nudged me and I spotted Suzie Sellhurst. She was the mother of the lad in the wheel chair and she made her way through the crowd and stretched up and scribbled out her husband's name on the sponsored walk poster and wrote her own. She nodded at a few of the regulars on her way out.

Sam looked along the line of pumps at me: there would be a sponsored streak poster on that wall before Wednesday night.

3

The lad in the wheelchair was fourteen year old Christopher Sellhurst. He had a tumour on his brain and spinal cord. A year ago he underwent major surgery, which had left him slightly disabled down the left hand side of his body. Since then, his condition had worsened and his family had been raising money for a treatment that was only available privately.

Last week, his father, Jack Sellhurst, dropped down dead.

Sam's night-in-shining-armour idea sounded great when we were in the bar. It gave us a real purpose to streak that we were sure would capture everyone's imagination. By the time we got back to the flat, though, we knew we couldn't do it. There just wasn't enough time to organise sponsorship before Wednesday's match, and the chances were, Sam would get caught, so if we said he was streaking for charity, it would be us that would benefit most from the publicity and not the charity. We sat up late, trying to figure out a way to drum up sponsorship and collect it, without revealing Sam's identity.

Monday morning.

The dream was the same as before, except when I ran down the pitch and veered off to the right, Jack Nicholson was walking across the pitch carrying something. I couldn't remember what, but I'm sure it was in a clear plastic bag.

When you see a famous person in a dream it can mean that 'you are observing a part of yourself that might hold that particular talent'. Being repeatedly chased in dreams means 'your subconscious is trying to make you aware of some important quality you need to realise and express in your life. Whoever is chasing you is the personification of that quality'. So, my subconscious – which previously had been guiding me along nicely – suddenly felt that Sam had an urgent quality that resided in me, and Jack Nicholson and I share a particular talent. Super. So another fifty Jack Nicholson dreams and I should be onto something.

I gave the *Jeremy Kyle Show* a miss, got ready and headed down to my mother's for some breakfast.

It was overcast, cold and windy.

I cut through town, past the playing fields and school and headed in the back way. My mother's house is an end terrace, two along from Sam's mother's.

My uncle Tommy was huddled next to the back door smoking.

Tommy's fifty-five, five-ten, with brushed back, light ginger and grey hair, like a Teddy Boy's, which he still dries by sticking his head half in the oven. Tommy has three vices: smoking – *twenty a day, probably less* – forty, no filter; drinking – *only a couple* – at least six pints a day; gambling – *Saturdays, odd one during the week if I've got a fancy for something* – every day. He once bet the full house-keeping on Norwich to beat West Ham. It was a Wednesday night and as his unsuspecting wife lay in the bath, Tommy paced the living room with the radio on low, phoning me every ten minutes. Norwich scraped a 1-0 win and Tommy lived like a king for a week.

Since his wife died a few years back, there's been no one to keep an eye on him except my mother. God only knows how much damage he does to himself now sat in front of his TV late at night.

Tommy was wearing a pair of old Rockport boots Sam had given him, blue worn out tracksuit bottoms and a three-quarter-length brown leather jacket from the charity shop. He turned around as I jumped over the fence into the garden.

'Morning, shit-face,' he said, discreetly nipping his roll-up.

'Morning, handsome.'

I gave him a cigarette and he snapped it in half and we lit up.

I unzipped my parka and sat on the garden bench.

Tommy sat next to me, elbows on his knees. His face was gaunt and unshaven, the scar around his neck bright red with the weather. He got that when he was twenty. He had been messing around with a shotgun with his friend and it had gone off, catching the side of his face and throat. The only visible damage now was the thick scar around his Adam's apple and a few pellets still embedded in his jaw line. My mother said he had become so nervous since that day. That was the day his left leg started to shake every time he sat down, causing merry hell at meal times.

He passed me *The Sun*. 'Sedgefield three o'clock, Al. Whatever you think.'

'Doubles and trebles?'

'Aye. If nowt comes to mind, we'll just go for the favourite.'

I've been gambling with Tommy since I was at school. My mother pretended to be annoyed, but she loved the bond between us. I remember when my mother found out I smoked. I was sixteen and it was becoming tiresome denying the cigarette dumps in the ashtray in my room were mine, so I came clean. My mother was devastated and immediately packed in smoking herself and has never touched one since. Tommy kept me in cigarettes the whole two weeks I was grounded.

'Did you get to the match, then?' he asked.

'Nah, I was working.'

'I thought the stripper might be you, but they say he's got a big knob.'

'Like me.'

He snorted and re-lit his rolly.

The back door opened and my mother rushed towards me with her arms outstretched. 'Alex! Darling! I never heard you come in!'

I bent down and she planted a smacker on my cheek.

'There's plenty of bacon in, I'm just going to the church meeting, it was put back because of the match. Did you go? What about that man? I tell you, the girls are going mad about him.' She stubbed Tommy's cigarette out on the wall without taking her eyes off me. 'I hope they're not over-working you at the pub, Alex. You need the free time to work on the book, that's the whole point of you being there. If you can't have free time, you might as well...'

My mother went off on one about me wasting my life.

When I was at uni, I entered a short story competition and won. It was published in the university mag and I got £25. Apparently, it was a big thing among the English students to win this competition. At the time, I was hardly attending any classes and was looking for a way out, so I told everyone I was leaving to write a novel.

That was over two years ago, and the lie is kind of getting out of control now. My mother thinks I'm on the last book of a trilogy, which I must submit by the end of the year. I recently downloaded the start of someone else's book from a writing website and gave it to her 'in confidence', to keep her off my back. I reckon I'm good for another six months before my career needs a change in direction, or Sam and I eventually get our act together and go travelling.

My mother gave me another kiss and went out the front door.

I went inside to make Tommy and me a bacon sandwich.

When I came out, Tommy was having a coughing fit. I got him a glass of water.

He straightened up and I handed him the water. There was blood down the side of his face and on his jacket sleeve.

'That doesn't look good,' I said.

He quickly wiped the blood off. 'It's nowt. It'll be them throat ulcers again. I'm in next week for a check-up anyway, but don't tell your mother, you know what she's like.'

We sat quiet for a while, eating our sarnies.

'I wish I knew who that stripper was,' Tommy said.

'Streaker. What for?'

'Every fucker in the club thinks they know who it is. I'd make a fortune.'

My mother's phone rang and I went inside to answer it. 'Hello.'

'Meet me at the flat in twenty minutes.' The line went dead.

It was quarter-past twelve, Sam's lunch hour.

'I'm doing a shoot,' I said.

'I'll follow you out. I'm going to the club. Just for a couple. I'm not drinking much these days.'

I pulled the front door behind us.

'Don't mention the doc's to your mother, will you?'

'I'll not, but take it easy, you'll lose those good looks.'

Tommy gave me the finger and I headed back to the flat.

Sam works in a printing factory during the day. He runs to work and back, so meeting me at lunchtime would mean another four mile run. I don't know how he could even contemplate it.

He was pacing the living room when I arrived.

'I've got it, Al. I've got it.'

I got past him and took my coat off and sat down.

Sam knelt in front of me. 'I'll streak on Wednesday at Darlington. No sponsorship, no nothing. No mention of the charity.'

'Eh? What's the point in that? I thought you were keen on the charity thing.'

'When I escape, it'll be all over the papers. Then we come out and say the next streak's for charity. That way we'd already be famous, and the charity benefits on the back of us. Not the other way round.'

'How do you propose getting out of Darlington's ground without getting caught? It'll be impossible.'

'If I get caught, I get caught. Who's bothered? If I don't, though, can you imagine the publicity?'

If the weekend had been anything to go by, Sam would be on the front of every newspaper, TV, Radio – everywhere.

'You see where I'm coming from,' he was saying,

kneeling down in front of me. 'We can't lose. And if I make it out, the next streak for charity will be the biggie. The swan song.'

'I swear, Sam, they'll make a film out of this if you get out of there.'

Sam was hyper.

I was worried.

'You'll have to sort the tickets today,' Sam was saying, standing at the front door. 'Just use my cash card.'

I needed to go to Darlington's ground. Plan his escape route. Find a bar close by to stash his clothes.

'And make sure they're as low down the stand as possible, so it doesn't take too long to get on the pitch.'

I couldn't believe he was going through with this.

'And, Al.' I lifted my head out of my hands. 'I've got you a date for Sunday night.'

I went to the window and shouted down to him. 'A date? Who with?' Sam took off. '*Sam! Who with!*'

4

Wednesday night

There were a few home supporters hanging around the ticket office as we approached Darlington's ground an hour before kick off. The 25,000 capacity stadium looked like a fortress with the blue turnstile doors locked shut beneath the white stanchions.

We walked around to the west stand, across the car park and out onto Neasham Road. Sam glanced back at the stadium as we reached the first houses, and again when we came to the Golden Fleece. We went inside.

The bar was packed with Darlington supporters.

We got a pint and stood in the corner and watched Sky Sports News on the big screen.

I got another round in and when I returned Sam was smirking.

'What's up?'

He shook his head and sipped his pint, still smirking.

'Nah, come on,' I said, 'let's have it.'

'Look in the mirror.'

I did. 'And?'

'Don't you think you look a bit peaky?'

I checked myself out again. 'Naff off.'

We'd hardly spoken since we left the flat, apart from to play, 'guess who your date for Sunday is'. And I already knew who it was.

'So,' Sam said. 'You reckon it's Becky.'

'It is Becky and you're taking the new secretary out, who probably wouldn't go on a straight date with you, so you've dragged me into. Admit it.'

'Might not be Becky – who, by the way, is looking extremely smart.'

'It's Becky.'

'What's wrong with Becky?'

'So it is Becky.'

'Not necessarily.'

'It's Becky. You're transparent.'

I met Becky last year at Sam's Christmas do. She's thirty-three, blonde, and as far as I can remember, small and skinny. Blonde, small and skinny Becky who was going through a divorce and ended up jammed in a doorway with me outside Newcastle Civic Centre waiting for her bus. She'd won a bottle of peach schnapps, which we downed, swig for swig. I can't remember leaving the doorway and for some reason, the next day, I bragged to Sam that I'd done allsorts with her. There's no way Sam would have kept that to himself at work and I felt really bad about it at the time.

'Worst comes to worst,' Sam was saying, 'you're going to get your leg over, aren't you? You're guaranteed that, and I swear, Al, she looks well tasty since she finished with her bloke.'

'And she's definitely up for it?'

He nodded, then took a deep breath when he realised the pub was emptying.

We followed the last supporters out and made for the ground.

There were queues of chanting fans at every turnstile.

Sam squeezed my shoulder, then headed for the north stand entrance. I joined the west stand queue and watched his blond head weaving through the crowd. Once inside, I stood against the back wall, out the way of people downing last-second pints. A father stood next to me with his two young sons. There were stewards on every exit.

Fat Boy Slim's *Right Here Right Now* blasted through the stadium, causing mass panic.

I was last up the stairs, my heart thumping.

The floodlit pitch was completely closed in, police and stewards around the perimeter and at the exits, 25,000 people on their feet cheering. There was no way Sam was running out of here.

I shuffled along row M and flopped onto my seat.

No matter what Sam had said, I knew getting caught wasn't an option for him. He had talked it up as being a laugh and that he wasn't bothered if he got caught – but he was. That's why he wore the mask in the first place. He'd done it so we could have a giggle watching it, not everyone else. I pictured him being dragged away, his mask ripped off, his head hanging limp.

There had only been twenty minutes played. I had

enough time to get to the north stand and stop him. I stood up and was about to leave when everyone around me jumped up, screaming for a penalty. The referee pointed to the spot.

Everyone remained standing and quietened down.

The Darlington player waited for the ref to blow, then coolly slotted the ball into the bottom left-hand corner. No sooner had the net bulged and Sam came tearing onto the pitch, twenty minutes earlier than we'd agreed.

I barged along the row, arms in the air, punching people out of the way, and threw myself down the stairs, just managing to grab the handrail as my feet went from beneath me. 'I've seen enough,' I panted at the steward as I fell towards him.

I sprinted through the car park, dodging between cars, come on, come on, you're going to make it, come on!

I burst through the side doors of The Golden Fleece and scrambled up the stairs and into the gents.

It was empty.

I kicked my shoes off and frantically pulled the second pair of jeans down to my ankles and tried to get the bastards off, but I couldn't get them past my stupid feet , so I dropped onto the floor, in among the piss and slops, and wriggled around until I got them off. I ripped the extra t-shirt over my head and stuffed the spare west stand ticket into the front pocket of the soaking jeans, rolled them up, and jammed them behind the cistern in the third cubicle along.

I calmed myself in the hallway, then went down into

the bar and ordered two pints.

A few minutes had passed when the side doors banged open and shut. Seconds later, four police and a couple of stewards ran past the window.

Sam, red-faced and blowing hard, joined me just as Darlington scored again. The place went up and we went ballistic, pints flying, over a table, on the floor, doing the pogo, we went off it and when Sam poured his pint over his own head, I was helpless to stop myself doing the same. Come on!

We were still throwing ourselves around when two police came in. No one paid them any attention and they soon left.

Unable to talk about it and frightened to leave, we knocked the pints and slammers back and sang our hearts out with the Darlington faithful.

Midway through the second half, we followed the majority of the supporters out and along the road towards the Copper Beech. Just as everyone ducked inside to catch the last ten minutes, Sam took off down the road at full speed.

I bolted after him, mimicking every shimmy and swerve, around lampposts, between cars, and across gardens and driveways. I was a good way behind when he disappeared into the train station.

I staggered down the stairs and collapsed onto the empty platform.

Sam appeared alongside me and we lay on our backs recovering.

I turned on my side and brought up a mouthful of beer.

Then another.

Sam got up and checked the timetable. 'Ten minutes.'

I looked up at him in total admiration. 'Can you believe it?'

He helped me up, then jerked me over his shoulder and ran the length of the platform, screaming, before dumping me on a seat and marching off, wired again.

I went after him. 'Well? Come on, then! What the hell were you thinking?'

'Unbelievable, Al. I swear, the crowd,' he shook his head. 'They give you so much.'

'Why did you go so early, you lunatic? I nearly didn't make it out in time.'

'It just built up and up and when he gave the penalty I was gripping the pants ready to go. I could've burst. And when you're out there, with the crowd, I can't explain.'

He said the players were stunned and the stewards and police slow to react, and even when it bottlenecked at the exit, he was going too fast for them to stop him.

'What about getting out downstairs? How did you get past the stewards?'

'I was nigh on jumping landing to landing, so when I hit the bottom, the steward right in front of me got a shock. It was a woman and she just stepped aside.'

I told him all about my part and the difficulty running in two pairs of jeans.

The train came and we got on. There was only a young skateboarder fidgeting with a ghetto blaster in our carriage.

I rested my head back against the window and pictured

Sam coming onto the pitch. Enclosed in a space with 25,000 people, all exits manned, and he ran into the centre of them, in the buff, then disappeared under their noses. There can't be many people in the world that would have the bottle to attempt that, and even less who could pull it of.

Sam nudged me and I rocked forward.

He nodded at the skateboarder, who was switching stations. 'Stick it back on Metro for a second, mate,' Sam said.

'.... Yes it can seem like good fun and a laugh at the time, but does it send out the right message? Do we want to take our children to football matches and be subject to a man exposing himself? Will he stop at this or is this the first stage in something more sinister? Is there a difference between this man exposing himself to thousands and a pervert jumping out of a bush and terrifying a girl on her way home from school?

'He's struck again tonight, listeners. The Faccome Flash. That's the subject of tonight's phone-in on the North East's number one, Night Owls...'

We legged it off the train at our stop and made for the flat.

5

In 1982 Erica Row bared her forty-inch chest at Twickenham and became an overnight phenomenon. Michael Angelo took to the pitch at Lords in 1975, hurdling the stumps, before being led away with his modesty covered by a police helmet, and Robert Opel (arguably the most famous of them all) caused a worldwide sensation when he streaked behind David Niven at the 1974 Oscars. Metro Radio DJ, Alan Robson, said that although these one-of incidents were probably spontaneous and just for laughs, the aftermath caused a lot of problems for authorities.

'The Darlington streaker is a different breed from all those I've mentioned,' he went on. 'He has evaded capture and wears a black sex mask. What does this tell us about the individual? Why hide if it's only fun? If it's not for fun, why do it? And the most frightening thing is that sexual predators could carry these masks and claim to be copycat streakers, and, from what I can see, the law can do very little about it. Until a serious crime is committed, that is. So what do we do? Hang around and wait for an outbreak of masked rapists or stop this man now?'

Sam had gone right into his shell and hadn't spoken for ages. What people thought about him meant a lot. Not because he's vain – which he is – but because of his father, who was a complete waster. An embarrassing waster, who drank himself to death before he was fifty. Sam's everything his father wasn't – fit, hardworking, and a good person. He tries too hard at times to be all three, and I know it's because he's bothered what people think. That's why he won't go travelling because he thinks people will see it as bumming around.

The first few calls had us rolling off our sofas.

Linda from South Shields. 'Alan, I'd just like to congratulate my sister who's lost two stone recently and also to say to The Flash, if he's listening, that I'm here for him, right now, touching myself...'

Julie from Byker. 'Alan, about the Flash. You're totally wrong about him. I know people who KNOW. You hear what I'm saying? They KNOW through experience that he's not a pervert, and I tell you, Alan, I'd do anything to get some of that...'

Peter from Darlington. 'Alan, pal, I was at the match tonight. Now, don't forget that we were playing Faccome, who are shit. It's a miracle they got the replay. Now, up until the penalty it was a dire affair. Absolute tripe. Now, when the kid came on, the atmosphere was electric. Electric, pal. And it stayed like that for the rest of the night. When do you get that being a Darlington fan? I'll tell you when, Alan. Never.

Never known, not like this. It's one of the best nights we've had and the kid got everyone going. Now, how can that be offensive, pal? I can't repeat what my missus is saying about him, but her and the kids think you're jealous and that you must have a tiny...'

Sam was well chilled now, sharing a smoke with me and guzzling the vodka.

It was after twelve o'clock when he staggered to the phone and slurred, 'I'm ringing in.'

I pushed myself up. 'You sure you don't want to leave it until tomorrow?'

Sam's face had collapsed and he had a vodka rash on his cheeks and neck.

Twenty minutes later, he was still standing with the phone in one hand, the vodka bottle in the other.

Robson snapped during one of the calls, when a woman said that she had just finished watching a phone video of the Flash's streak at Faccome and was heading to the radio station with her 'satched' knickers. 'Enough!' he yelled. 'Enough! The debate ends here! Vulgarity is not what this show's about. We won't be taking any calls on streaking, nudity or anything associated with it.' There was a long pause, then, 'After the break, it's dedications and announcements only.'

After some dedications with smutty tag-ons, a seventy-year-old woman came on to talk about her late husband, on the anniversary of his death, and his relevance to tonight's show. She said he was a great man, 'big as a bear and just as hairy'. He had been a high-ranking officer in the Navy and had run a successful stationary business. They had many friends and she couldn't have asked for more sincere well-wishers when he died, but the unrelenting support came from their friends at Heddon-on-the-Wall Naturist Club, where they had been members all their married life. She felt closest to her husband when nude, and although the walks were getting too much now, she was happy serving up the tea and biscuits.

The woman wasn't at all fazed being on the radio. Her speech was slow and deliberate and quite soothing. When she'd been speaking a while she sounded croaky and stopped for a drink. She had been on a good ten minutes, when Robson started steering her to a finish.

'I'm still enjoying life, Alan,' she said, 'but not half as much without Bobby. This young lad streaking reminds me of him. Full of fun, running around in the nuddy. Bobby loved the fun. Anyway, I'm off to bed. God bless.'

Robson went straight to the adverts.

After the break, he called out the Faccome Flash.

'I don't, and never will, agree with what this man is doing. I won't try to pretend that I understand the reaction of the public to him, either. What I will do is continue to serve this community the best way I know how. So if you're listening, Streaker, ring the show on this separate number, and tell us why you're doing this. Better still, let us at Metro know your identity, proving that you don't have a hidden agenda.'

Sam felt his way along the wall towards the

bathroom. 'Ring it, I'm going to spew.'

The line was constantly engaged.

Sam came out the bathroom, his face ash white, and reached for the vodka bottle. 'Try, ring-back.'

I did and got through and instantly chucked him the phone like it had burst into flames.

I turned the stereo off and darted into my bedroom and switched my clock radio on.

Robson was explaining to a woman the perils of supporting this streaker, when he interrupted their conversation to say, as far as they could make out, they had the person who had streaked at Faccome on Saturday, and Darlington tonight, on the line.

'You've obviously been listening to the show, so you've heard what I think, and it appears that I'm in the minority in opposing what you've been doing. So, for us all to get a better understanding, tell me from the beginning how this all came about.'

There was a ridiculously long pause and I held my breath, hoping Sam hadn't choked up, or worse, fell asleep.

'First of all I'd just like to thank everyone who has phoned in and supported me tonight.' His voice was deep and controlled. 'Especially the Darlington fans. You were great tonight. You made me feel ten feet tall, and I can tell you now if the next lot of supporters are anything like you, there's no chance I'll get caught.'

A woman clapped and cheered in the studio.

'It's all very well thanking everyone, but where the hell do you get off thinking it's acceptable to expose yourself to families on a night out supporting their local team? Exposing yourself is against the law. And why the mask?'

Another decent pause, then, 'You asked me on this show, so either hear me out or I hang up.'

The delayed responses were cranking up the suspense and mystery. You didn't know if you were going to hear from him again or not, and I, no doubt like everyone else listening, was hanging on his every word.

'I'm doing this for a very good cause and tonight was instru... instrumm... tonight was vital in getting the publicity needed for it to be a success.' Sam composed himself after the stutter. 'Tonight was a dummy run. A week on Saturday I'm going to streak at one of the North East's top three venues. Sunderland, Newcastle or Middlesborough.'

Robson snorted, 'Well, at least you'll be caught, no matter what your reasons.'

'You want to put your money where your mouth is, Mr Robson? In the name of charity, how much are you willing to stick down that I don't make it out of one of those stadiums a week Saturday?'

'What charity? You're talking nonsense. You're a drunk exhibitionist clutching at straws because you're being exposed on live radio -'

'Christopher Sellhurst needs an operation and this'll hopefully bring in the money he needs to go private.'

'Who's Chrisopher Sellhurst? Why the sex mask? Why won't you reveal yourself to us?'

'I'd be grateful for any contribution towards this charity.'

'How can people sponsor a criminal act? You haven't thought this one through, have you?'

'Who mentioned sponsorship? Support, not sponsorship.' Sam was slurring now and his sentences tailing off. 'If any female fans would like a date with me, send your details with your donation to enter a free draw, to the Fiddler's Arms in Faccome.'

'You're talking gibberish. This isn't about charity, it's about your ego, of which I've heard enough. After the break, your reactions to the man exposing himself to children for charity, on the North East's number one, Night Owls.'

I walked back out into the living room, shell-shocked, that not only had he told the world about the charity, but that he'd offered to whore himself out in a raffle.

Sam had passed out on the sofa clutching the phone to his chest.

I lit up and listened to the rest of the show.

6

The phone was ringing. I rolled off the sofa and staggered into my room.

The dream. I was giving Becky one from behind, at the living room window, with the blinds fully opened. It was dark and I could see someone pointing up at us from the pavement. Becky was waving and I joined in, totally unbothered at being spotted.

... Sam was carrying something in a clear plastic bag. I kept trying to have a look, but he held it close to his side. The motorway lights were blinding. I thought we were playing chicken, but Sam tripped me over and held me down. I stopped struggling and he lay next to me. Cars came from behind us, screeching and sounding their horns. Any second one was going to go over us. I kept my eyes shut and elbows tucked tight into my sides as another shadow passed and a horn sounded. Sam was wafting the plastic bag above my face, something red and silver or gold.

... We were walking towards our flat. I looked up and Becky was leaning out the window, rocking back and forth, laughing. I crossed the road and stopped to let a bus pass and I stared at the driver – a young Jack

Nicholson, laughing.

I downed the glass of water that had been on my bedside table for days, then ringed the reccurring elements in the dream. Sam, Jack Nicholson, and the bag with something gold in it. Sam, Jack, the bag. And gold. Because there were reccurring elements in my dreams, it meant my subconscious was trying to get an important message to me.

You only have three seconds after you wake to remember your dream. REM sleep is when most dreams occur. If you are awoken during REM sleep – which is when you first fall asleep and start dreaming and the eyes flicker – you will remember much more of your dream. The longer the REM sleep lasts, the longer the dream. I needed to stay sober and wake myself during REM sleep.

I went into the living room.

Sam was still out of it.

I checked out the window, the sky was dark grey and it was raining hard. The queue at the bus stop was dotted with bright coloured brollies.

I made us both a coffee and kicked Sam's feet as I came back in.

He stirred, then slowly sat up.

'Well, well, well,' I said. 'If it isn't the Mighty Flash, who likes to do a lot of work for charity.'

I handed him the coffee.

'I feel ill.'

'You don't say.'

'Is there any -' he went to stand up, then held his head with his finger tips and sat back down. 'Fizzy pop, Al.'

I got him a Diet Coke.

'So,' I said. 'No work?'

He shook his head.

'Not even a little promotional work for your forth coming mercy streak?'

'What you on about?'

'Don't tell me you can't remember your star performance on the Night Owls?'

Sam was sitting forward, massaging his eyes with the heels of his palms. 'We didn't get through, did we?'

I went through his finest hour in detail, finishing with the raffle. 'Your exact words were, "I haven't had it for a while, Alan, so the winner will be in for a right good night, if you know what I mean, mate".'

Sam dashed into the bathroom and violently threw up.

He retched a couple more times, then washed up, before coming back out, full of purpose. 'You're talking shite,' he said. 'It's coming back. I mentioned the Darlington fans, didn't I?'

On the plus side, the listeners loved him and every woman in the northeast wanted to bed him. And why should he be that bothered if he embarrassed himself when no one knew who he was?

'What if someone sussed my voice?'

'Unlikely, didn't even sound like you.'

He lifted his hand, 'I remember, it's coming back,

that arsehole Robson saying I was a paedophile. That's what sent me off on one.'

'He didn't say that. He just went on about the mask and you exposing yourself to children.'

'Did I really offer to shag whoever won the raffle?'

I nodded. 'In a sleazy, muffled voice, you said something about unleashing your sex- starved python.'

Sam dropped to his knees laughing and rolled onto his back, hysterical.

His laughing fit got me going and I ended up face down on the sofa, smacking the cushion with one hand and holding my gut with the other. The radio, getting out of the stadium last night, and him – of all people – making a tit of himself, was too much, and in the end I had to leave the room.

Standing in the kitchen, I held onto the bench top, taking deep breaths, trying desperately not to start giggling, then I thought of something and went back in.

'What if a bloke wins the raffle?'

The two of us were silently laughing so hard that all you could hear was the occasional yelp as we gasped for air. The captions for a gay streaker were endless, but I couldn't get the words out for laughing.

We marched off into separate rooms.

We tried coming back out twice, but just being in the same room set us off again.

We eventually got on speaking terms, but Sam kept saying, 'Seriously though, did I say....' *Seriously though*, was doing me right in and I had to ban the words from his vocabulary.

I switched the TV on, just in time to catch *The Jeremy Kyle Show*.

The Jeremy Kyle Show is the best morning show I've ever seen. It's similar to the Jerry Springer Show, except it's big on emotion and not violence. I think I've seen one fight in all the time I've been watching it. Jeremy Kyle's about five-seven, early forties, with short brown hair tufted up at the front, and was a DJ for over ten years. The best thing about *The Jeremy Kyle Show* is Jeremy Kyle. He gets so emotionally involved, you'd think he was a member of the guest's family. I've seen him hell-bent on giving some skunk-smoking lay-about a hard time because he does nothing for his young family – they're usually seventeen-to-twenty-year-olds with two kids – only to change his mind halfway through when the lad bears his soul and Jeremy sees beyond the paranoia and black broken teeth that he really does love his family and has lost his way due to his dope addiction. By this stage, Jeremy is dramatically dishing out his words of wisdom and the importance of doing it FOR THE KIDS. It's always for the kids.

I thought the guests must be on a fortune to reveal all about themselves and their families, but apparently it's the specialist help they receive after the show that's the attraction. The format of the show's like this: Jeremy Kyle chats to the person with the gripe first and makes sure they know how they feel towards the accused – no change of heart because they're on TV. He then brings them together on stage and somehow gets them to argue like they were back home in their own living room. I remember when a young teenage son with an anger problem started arguing with his father because his father had stolen his cigarettes that morning. The kid stormed off and punched a wall and the father sat back with a 'told you so' look on his face, and the mother went after the son. In just a few minutes, you knew them so well and what everyday life was like for them.

Today's show was: HAS MY MUM HAD A BABY WITH MY HUSBAND!

The daughter was eighteen, had two kids to her boyfriend and was six months pregnant. The mother had a two-year-old daughter, which the older daughter believed her boyfriend had fathered.

Sam always takes the piss when I mention the show, saying it's staged and that I'll be watching wrestling next. Today, he was rooting for the daughter and slagging the mother off.

Just as they were about to announce the DNA results, the phone rang.

'Just leave it!' Sam snapped.

I went and answered it.

'Hello.'

It was a woman with a squeaky voice asking for Sam.

'Em, who's calling?'

'Is that Alex?'

'Eh, yeah, who's this?'

'Cagey or what? It's Becky! From Sam's place!'

I cleared my throat and straightened up. 'Becky! How goes it?'

'Not bad, not bad. You sound rough, heavy night?'

'Sort of.'

'Look, I've just been asked to find out if Sam's okay. He's not turned in. Is he all right?'

'Yeah, well no, he's a bit…'

'Hung over. Don't worry, I'll cover for him. So… '

Sam was shouting at the TV, oblivious that work was on the phone.

'So,' I said. 'You, eh, you up for the weekend, then?'

She went quiet. 'The weekend? What's happening at the weekend?'

I held my hand over the receiver and hissed at Sam. 'Hoy! Wanker!'

Sam held his hand up to silence me.

I could have killed him. It was Thursday and the bastard hadn't even asked her yet.

I took my hand off the receiver and stammered, 'Eh, I'm getting crossed wires I think.'

'Of course I'm looking forward to the weekend! I can't wait! What about you? We're going to have a good night, or what?'

I'd forgotten just how lively Becky was. At the Christmas party, she was dragging me up to dance every two minutes and drinking anything she could get her hands on. It was only when *I've had the time of my life* came on, that I declined and made for the door and she ran after me and launched herself onto my back, clutching her bottle of schnapps.

'So you're definitely up for it?'

'Why wouldn't I be? You haven't had that lovely hair cut, have you?'

'I've got a skinhead now.'

'No, you haven't. Look I'll have to go, the boss is coming. See you Sunday, bye-bye.'

I hung up.

After *The Jeremy Kyle Show*, we sat on our sofas in silence.

After a while Sam said, 'I'm going to do it, Al.'

'You don't have to. No one knows it was you last night. And you don't owe the Sellhursts a thing. We don't even know them.'

Sam was doing this to prove to himself that he was who he thought he was. He'd risk humiliating himself and his mother to find out for sure that he was nothing like his father. If it took something as extreme as this to convince him, then so be it.

We went to get dressed.

When I came back, Sam was standing at the mirror adjusting his beanie. 'What did you say before last night's streak?'

I shook my head.

'If I get out of the stadium they'll make a film out of it.' He rested a hand on my shoulder. 'Al, even if we don't make it out this time they'll make a film out of it – starring you and me.'

He was right.

'Imagine,' I said.

'Imagine. Throw the charity angle in and everyone's a winner.'

I went into the kitchen to check the phone book for the Sellhurst's address.

When I came back he was reading my dream journal.

'Giving Becky one from behind. Nice.'

I snatched it off him.

'I can't believe you're still pissing about with that dream shit.'

I pulled my parka on. 'Shit, is it? How come you slog your guts out in a sweat shop all day and have no money, and I don't, and have no money?'

'Because you're bone-idle and scrounge off your mother and I prefer to graft and pay my way.'

'Because I'm in tune with my subconscious and know what's right for me.' We made for the door. 'At least, I was until all this started.'

We went out into the pouring rain and headed for the West Layton estate.

7

The rain had stopped by the time we reached the West Layton estate. We stood on the corner of the Sellhurst's street next to a small graffitied sub-station.

The street was empty, except for four teenagers hanging around at the far end next to the school fence. The houses were prefab terraces with metal cladding and two foot high concrete garden walls. The house numbers had been crudely painted on the garden walls and dustbins.

Sam was scraping his shoe on the kerb. 'So you're happy to decide your career path based on what you can suss out from your dreams, even though you admit there's no way of knowing for sure if you're doing it right?'

'Life path. It's not just about work. It's about your whole psyche and tapping into your subconscious. And what I said was, there's no guarantee that a person is analysing their dreams properly, no matter which method they use if they're not being totally honest.'

The kids were getting curious and had moved along the fence towards us.

'What if you can't remember any of your dreams?'

'What, never?'

Sam shook his head.

'That's because you're too hyper. You don't chill out enough.'

The teenagers were nearly upon us, so we made for number sixty-five.

The Sellhursts lived on a corner. A bare, waist-height privet ran the full perimeter of the garden. The front garden was covered in small white stones right up to the window, and the side garden was patchy grass. The concrete path leading to the front door was cracked in places and had fallen away.

Neither of us made a move towards the door.

Sam said, 'So you reckon if I wake up during this REM sleep I'll remember something?'

I nodded. 'Without doubt. But you can't base everything on one dream, you need to record loads.'

The Sellhurst's front door opened and Suzie Sellhurst stepped out and leant against the doorframe and folded her arms. Suzie Sellhurst was about five-four, late forties, slim, and had short black hair parted at the side, which fell partly over her right eye. She was wearing a green and white check *Asda* tabard over a pink t-shirt and skin-tight bleached jeans. She had deep lines either side of her mouth that disappeared when she couldn't hold her smile back any longer.

'Come on in, boys,' she said in a husky voice. 'I've been expecting you.'

We followed her inside and along the narrow

passageway and into the kitchen.

The kitchen was small and bare and white. Apart from the rustling of our coats, the house was silent.

Suzie stood at the back door and took a draw of the cigarette that had been burning in the ashtray, then stubbed it out.

Sam and I spread out a little and unbuttoned our coats.

Suzie, arms folded and biting her bottom lip, said, 'Come on then, put a girl out of her misery. Which one of you is it?'

Sam pulled his beanie off and ruffled his hair. 'Which one do you think?'

I straightened up.

Suzie coyly twisted from side to side and looked us both up and down.

Her eyes settled on Sam. 'Tell me it's you, Blondie.'

Sam swept her off her feet and over his shoulder and ran out the back door. He sprinted up the garden, round the washing line post, and zigzagged back. Suzie was still screaming when he set her down on the step and came back inside. She stood at the back door, dramatically fanning her face with both hands. 'If I was ten years younger,' she panted. 'No, make that five.'

Suzie Sellhurst was in her forties and hadn't aged particularly well.

Suzie Sellhurst was attractive – especially when she spoke.

Suzie Sellhurst – once she knew who HE was – was so attracted to him she could hardly look him in the face.

Christopher was shouting from his room.

Suzie went to see to him.

After a few minutes, she wheeled her son through the tight openings and into the kitchen.

Christopher was completely bald. His hands, neck, face and head, were all the same unblemished pink colour. He looked like a huge baby, too big for a pram.

Suzie knelt in front of him. 'You'll never guess who this is?'

Christopher looked up at both of us and shook his head.

She nodded at Sam. 'The Faccome Flash.'

His mouth opened and kept on opening, like a drawbridge, until we could see his tonsils.

Sam did a mock run on his tiptoes around the tiny kitchen and grabbed Christopher's arms and gently punched the air with them.

Christopher eventually let out a squeal that I thought was never going to end.

Suzie choked up and turned away and reached for her cigarettes.

Sam knelt down and talked football with Christopher.

I joined Suzie at the door and lit up and started telling her our plans.

Suzie insisted on hearing our story from the start. I told her about the first streak and then seeing her in the bar altering the sponsored walk poster. I told her about last night and she was in stitches at how we'd escaped. I wanted to tell her that we weren't superheroes and were doing this as much for ourselves as we were for Christopher. I wanted to talk the situation down and treat any success as a bonus. Instead, I told her we expected huge publicity after last night's radio show and that Brian at the Fiddler's was backing our campaign and would be dealing with all the sponsorship and donations. Sam chipped in and said he was picking the posters up tonight and was going to try for corporate sponsorship by advertising on his body.

I can't ever remember either of us running off at the mouth like this before and if Christopher hadn't interrupted us, God knows what we would have said.

'Mam, Mam, Mam, he's going to streak at Newcastle next!'

'What's that?' Sam said, checking Christopher's fixture list.

I mumbled, 'Eh, definitely Newcastle, is it?'

'Got to be, they're the only ones playing at home. Here, look.'

'Oh, yes,' Sam said, in too deep a voice. 'The mighty Toon Army.'

I couldn't believe what I was hearing or saying.

I was desperate to get out of there and after Sam had promised to drop the posters off tonight so Suzie could distribute them first thing tomorrow along with the collection buckets, we made for the door.

We jogged along the street, heads down against the rain, occasionally turning back to wave, until we

reached the substation.

'Shit shit shit shit shit shit!'

Sam grabbed me by the shoulders. 'Fucking Newcastle, Al. Fucking Newcastle!'

The two of us marched back and forth across the road throwing our arms up in the air like a couple of air traffic controllers malfunctioning, barking single words at each other: *posters, Newcastle, tomorrow…*

The rain was stotting off the pavement.

Tickets, Brian, police…

The surface water was up to our ankles.

Newcastle, posters, tomorrow…

A car came round the corner and snapped us out of it and we started down the bank, looking for shelter. The first bus stop was full, so we kept on running.

Sam hung a left along a lane and stood tight up against a wall.

I joined him.

It was so dark it could have been midnight.

We stood there in silence for ages.

The rain never let up.

Sam said. 'I could try and do the posters tonight.'

We walked through the pothole puddles and out onto the bank.

'I could see Brian. See what he says.'

Sam nodded.

An old woman, hunched over and dressed as a yellow polka dot umbrella, was struggling along the pavement towards the bus stop. The bus was coming and she wasn't going to make it. Sam went over to the woman and I stood on the road and flagged the bus down. The driver indicated to pull over and I suddenly felt short of breath. I stepped back. Sam helped her on and as it pulled away, I quickly looked at the driver: it wasn't Jack Nicholson or anyone who looked like him.

We kept on walking.

'What was wrong back there?' Sam asked.

I shook my head.

'Didn't look like nothing. Did you recognise that driver?'

I didn't answer.

We reached town and stood under the canopy of the Fruit and Veg shop.

People were dashing from shop to shop and huddled in doorways waiting for buses.

The coffee shop window was steamed up.

'How are we going to get tickets for a Man U game?' I asked

'There's two for sale on the board at work. We only need one more.'

Sam turned towards me. 'It's possible, Al.'

I shook my head.

'Honestly, I'm telling you with that crowd behind me, the adrenaline.'

'I'm not worried about you,' I said. 'I could be in row Z and have to make it a mile down the road in two pairs of jeans on a second's notice.'

'Why don't you do some training?' he said, smirking. 'Say, a mile uphill in your gear.'

I gave him the finger.

'Seriously, why not?'

'Because I'll look like I've shit myself for starters.' I pulled my hood down. 'I'll tell you what. If I'm doing all the shit, I want you to do something for me.'

'Shit?'

'Dreams. Tomorrow. Wake each other during REM and record our dreams.'

'No bother. Even if you're engaging in a sex act, do you want waking?'

'Especially, that way I'll remember it.'

Sam ran to work and I went into the Fiddler's to see Brian.

8

Brian was sitting in his office with the door open, reading a letter. Light from the side window cut across him and it looked like a salt bomb had been detonated on the crown of his head. The dandruff had spread through the black curls and reached his shoulders. Brian was in the only clothes I'd ever seen him in, white shirt, black waistcoat, black pants. He was smoking.

I gently knocked on the door. 'Aye, aye.'

The folds of flesh above his eyelids momentarily lifted.

I sat in the chair opposite and waited for him to finish.

He slid the letter towards me. The manager of The Fiddler's Arms wasn't returning and they wanted to interview Brian for the post.

'Nice one,' I said, handing the letter back. 'You stand a good chance, Brian, the takings have been through the roof since you arrived.'

He walked over to the safe and took out a large red ledger book and dropped it on his desk. 'What if they ask to see that?'

It was a record of supplies.

'You're only a week behind.'

He nodded at the open safe, where there were four other books.

Brian said they also wanted him to give a presentation.

'On what?'

He shrugged.

'Well, did they not say? Is it about how you're going to run the pub? Or your past experience, or what?'

He picked the letter up again, vacantly staring at it, like he still couldn't believe what was written on it.

I got up and took one of his cigarettes and sat on the windowsill with my foot up on the chair. I lit up and opened the top window.

It was still chucking it down.

I finished the cigarette, then said, 'How long's it been since you worked in a bar?'

He blew his cheeks out and leant back, hands behind his head. 'A good few years.'

I nodded.

'What was the last pub you worked at?'

He stretched back again, blowing hard. 'Red Lion.'

I waited for him to elaborate.

He didn't so I asked him which Red Lion.

He stared straight ahead.

I waited.

And waited.

Nothing.

'You've not worked in a pub before, have you?'

Brian looked down at the letter and rubbed the stubble either side of his chin. After a while, he glanced up at me, then reached under his desk and brought out a bottle of whisky and two glasses.

A couple of years ago, after losing his job, Brian ended up on the government NEW DEAL scheme, which trains over thirty-fives. He wanted to go back into insurance, but accepted placements at Marks and Spencer, Rentokil, The Ministry and Walcock's Bar Furniture.

After refusing a placement at Fenwicks, Brian had to look for full-time work or he wouldn't receive benefit. He stated on his CV that his last position was Manager of Walcock's Bar Furniture, and sent it to agencies looking for admin work. A week later he got the call to cover at The Fiddler's.

'Thought I might get kept on if things went well,' he said, pouring himself another.

I told him that all he'd have to do to get kept on as barman was stick himself on the staff rota. That perked him right up and he gave himself another shot of whisky, which went straight down the hatch, followed by a shudder and a rub of the hands. I also offered to help him update the books and prepare for Wednesday's presentation. Each piece of good news was welcomed with a tipple of whisky and rub of the hands. After draining another glass, he re-filled mine and tossed me his last cigarette.

'Actually,' I said, exhaling smoke towards the top

window, 'I'm after a bit of a favour myself – which, as it happens, also benefits you.'

The folds of flesh above the eyes lifted again as he prepared to receive more good news.

'Now, I don't know if you've heard about last night's radio show, have you?'

He pointed at the phone on his desk. 'I've had to take it off the hook. Women've been ringing up every five minutes wanting to buy raffle tickets. I was going to ask, you, about it.' He cocked his head and gave me a peculiar look, like he could hear a high-pitched sound somewhere, then said, 'You're not him, are you?'

'I wish. It's Sam.'

'Ahhh,' he said, tapping his pockets looking for cigarettes. 'Thought it might be Sam.'

I told him about visiting the Sellhursts and the planned streak next Saturday and that we needed his help to collect the donations. Nothing was a problem to Brian, who was more concerned about finding some cigarettes.

'Mind, you'll have a job keeping it quiet,' he said, raking through the desk drawers.

'How's that?'

'There's already been people asking questions.'

'Who?'

'Bloke been in the bar since we opened, asking about The Flash and what a great thing it is. Newspaper man, if you ask me.'

I stood up and suddenly felt mortal drunk. 'Issss he still in?'

He shrugged.

'What'sss he look like?'

'You'll not miss him.'

I shoulder-charged the doorframe on the way out and felt my way along the dark corridor and into the bar.

The old-timers were in the far corner under a cloud of smoke playing dominoes and watching the racing channel. The stranger was sat close by, reading The Times. He was tall and carrot ginger and wearing a smart grey suit. His overcoat was on the chair next to him. He looked up as I came in.

I acknowledged the regulars then sat at the bar with my back to them. The barman went on his break and Brian took over.

Brian poured us both a whisky.

'What do you think?' he whispered.

I glanced over my right shoulder just as the bloke looked up and we both nodded. I turned back and he folded his newspaper and picked his coat up. He came over and leant on the bar and ordered a lager shandy. He looked like the Gingerbread Man in a suit and I wanted to rugby tackle him to the floor and ask him who he was working for and tie him up and leave him in Brian's office until after next Saturday.

He asked Brian for a dash of lime.

I downed the whisky, then blurted out, 'So where you from?'

'Sorry?'

'You're not local, are you?'

'I'm not, no. Up from York. On business.'

'Ah,' I said, 'York. on business.'

A long pause.

'I take it you're local, though.'

I was trying to peel the back off the beer mat without tearing it. 'Yeah, yeah.'

'So, do you work here?'

'Head barman. Shit.' I'd ripped the beer mat in half.

Next thing I knew, he was back in his seat pretending to read the paper.

I sloped out back to have a word with Brian.

'Keep an eye on him and anyone else acting sssuspicious,' I said, struggling into my parka. 'And not a word to anyone about anything.'

Brian tapped his nose. 'I'll ring you if anything happens.'

I patted his shoulder and went out the side door and around the front and stood at the bus stop.

The Gingerbread Man was watching me. He raised his glass.

I sharply looked away and marched off towards home.

9

I woke up on the sofa at four o'clock and didn't feel too rough. I made a coffee and stuck a frozen pizza in the oven and watched Deal or No Deal. When it had finished, I unplugged the phone, brought the clock radio from my room, and set it for one hour and twenty minutes time, to hopefully wake me during REM sleep. I lit the oil burner, stuffed cotton wool in my ears, and drank a glass of warm milk, before falling asleep.

*

Sam was shaking me. He mouthed, Are you deaf?

I pulled the cotton wool out. 'What time is it?'

He was still wearing his beanie and denim jacket. 'One in the morning. What's that smell?'

'What smell?'

'What smell? Are you for real? That flowery, puffy smell.'

I pointed at the burner. 'Lavender. It encourages restful sleep.'

So restful I couldn't remember a thing.

I checked the alarm time on the clock radio.

'Well then?' he said, standing to the side.

The poster on the wall above the fireplace was a cartoon of The Faccome Flash. Against a red background, he was wearing a black mask with black and white tassels and a huge gold star covered his modesty. Across the top in gold, THE FACCOME FLASH RIDES AGAIN! Underneath in smaller capitals, CHRISTOPHER SELLHURST CHARITY. Across the bottom, in white, NEWCASTLE UNITED v MANCHESTER UNITED 29TH NOVEMBER. Halfway down on the right hand side, just above his elbow, BACK ME TO BEAT THE BOBBIES, PLEASE GIVE GENEROUSLY. ALL DONATIONS TO THE FIDDLER'S ARMS, FACCOME.

I was transfixed by the hooded superhero staring back at me, hands on hips, chest puffed up, catch me if you can.

'Jesus, Sam, I can't believe we're doing this.'

'I've already delivered the posters to Suzie.'

'We're doing it, aren't we?'

'We're doing it,' he said, walking away.

'We're doing it,' I repeated, walking after him.

Sam tossed me a bottle of vodka and I went back and stood in front of the poster.

The Flash was like a monument staring down at us, willing us on.

Sam had taken his jacket and beanie off. 'I'll make it out of there. You watch.'

My heart was pounding as I pictured the fans screaming for him and me taking off down the stairs.

'Imagine,' Sam whispered.
'Imagine.'
We settled down on our sofas and flicked the TV on.

10

Friday Morning.

I walked into the living room with a coffee and pulled the blinds up and opened the window, letting in sunshine and a freezing cold breeze. I switched the TV on and got into *This Morning*. The phone-in was about domestic violence and the guest was a twenty-four-year-old woman, who I'd read about in the papers. She had met her boyfriend at work, a week after joining a new company. Within a month they were engaged. She said he was possessive, but she didn't feel threatened by him physically. One day, she was off work ill and her fiancé came home and said he had a surprise for her and ran her a bath. After a long soak she got out and got dressed. He told her to get back in the bath and get ready for the surprise. Once she was comfortable, he ran into the bathroom and tried to electrocute her by throwing a hairdryer, lamp and stereo into the bath. When that didn't work, he jumped into the bath and forced her head under the water. She played dead and he left her lying there. When she got out, he was waiting on the stairs and panicked, saying it was a joke, even though he'd locked all the doors and windows. The lad got sentenced to nine years.

On the adverts I made another coffee, then came back in and leant out the window to have a smoke. There were a handful of people at the bus stop, still in winter coats and jackets. It was clear blue skies and I could see the rooftops of the estates on the other side of the flyover for miles. I leant out a bit further and looked right and I could see inland towards Newcastle, houses and roads and patches of terracotta roofs where new estates had been built, and fields – one brown, one green, one brown, one green. The other way, towards town, housing estates either side of the motorway, four blocks of flats, more houses – no terracotta roofs around here, the glassworks chimney, then the sky meeting the sea – blue meets grey. I looked down before flicking my cigarette dump and there were three other residents, spaced out along the block, hanging out, enjoying the weather.

The regional news was on so I started my stretching programme. Stretching three to four times a day encourages lucid dreaming. Lucid dreaming is dreaming when you know you are dreaming, like when you're waking up and you don't want to and you turn over and get back into the dream, although it's never quite as good as before. Leaving notes around the house reminding yourself to lucid dream and saying it out loud and taking plenty of power naps also helps. The better you get at lucid dreaming, the more control you have over your dreams.

I stretched up, nearly touching the ceiling, then slowly brought my arms down to my sides. I opened my legs and stretched to the side, left hand to left ankle – well, as far as I could, then the other side. Bending at the waist, I let my head and arms hang forwards and stayed there for thirty seconds before straightening up.

I moved my legs further apart and fell forward onto my palms. I steadied myself, and was about to walk my hands back towards me when I heard, 'And the locals are one hundred percent behind this mystery streaker, who has already escaped twice from football grounds in the past week'. The female presenter was outside the Fiddler's.

I scrambled over the coffee table and plugged the phone in.

Eleven messages. Sam, Switch Metro on, I'm on Tony Horn in twenty minutes. Sam, did you get the message? Sam, for fuck's sake take the cotton wool out! Brian, in a whisper, it's me, you better come down before I open up. Sam, Christ's sake, Al, ring as soon as. Brian, You Know Who is in again, you better come down.

The phone started beeping so I stopped listening to the messages and answered it.

'Yeah.'

'Where the fuck you been?'

'I forgot the phone was unplugged, we've just been on the news.'

'Get down the Fiddler's, Brian's been on, he's struggling to hold it together.'

'What happened with the radio?'

'Hurry on, Al, he's bricking it about his bosses coming down.'

'On my way.'

The town was packed out, but quiet, with everyone busying themselves at the market stalls. There were women in Asda uniforms dotted around shaking red buckets, and with every step I heard, The Flash... The Flash... The Flash...

Brian was in his office and looked up when I came along the corridor.

'Have you seen?'

I unbuttoned Sam's denim jacket and took it off. 'It is market day, you know.'

'The cameras I mean. They've been in here asking questions as well.'

I took one of his cigarettes and sat on the windowsill. 'What did you tell them?'

'Nothing, I've been in here all morning answering the phone and keeping out the road and,' he pointed at a pile of colourful boxes in the corner, 'opening them.'

I walked over and picked a black vibrator up off the floor. The tag attached to the end had *forever yours* written on it and two kisses. Using a pencil, I lifted a pair of knickers out of the wrapping papers and cautiously brought them towards my nose, then flicked them away. Vibrators, knickers, all-in-ones, pouches, leather, plastic, masks, cuffs, whips, photos, DVDs, which I'd be examining later, bottle of liquor, box of shortbread, male nude playing cards, lucky dip lottery ticket for next Saturday, a toffee hammer and MONEY. We put the gifts to one side until we could think of something to do with them and I boxed the letters, photos and DVDs.

Brian had conveniently stacked the record books from the safe on his desk and had opened one, ready to get started. He said the brewery had been on after hearing about it all on TV and they wanted him to maximise the pub's involvement to ensure that the people came to the Flash's rightful home. Brian casually placed a carrier bag full of receipts next to my chair on his way out.

*

'If it isn't David Copperfield hard at it,' Sam said, peering round the door.

I pushed the book away. 'You're going to have to muck in with this.'

Sam picked the black vibrator up. 'You reckon this is for me or her?'

'Who knows,' I said, joining him. 'There're some cracking photos, though.'

Sam examined the pile with his foot and picked the toffee hammer up.

'What do you reckon?'

'Haven't a clue.'

Brian came in, out of breath and sweating. 'You're going to have to come out, we can't cope and Ginger's back.'

Sam steered him towards the door. 'Fear not, the A-team are here.'

We followed him into the bar and were greeted by a heaving sea of red faces singing Queen's *Don't Stop Me Now*. Sam hopped up onto the bar and, arms outstretched, announced that he was the Faccome Flash. The women, crazy-eyed, makeup all over and clutching bottles of Budweiser and vodka chasers, surged towards him and both side entrance doors were forced open and punters spilled out onto the street. Sam worked the crowd, high-fiving the men and leaning over the bar and kissing the women, all the while collecting fivers and tenners and stuffing them into the nearest collection bucket.

An old school mate's mother, in her fifties and just hanging onto her looks, kept seductively and not so seductively sticking her tongue out at me. When it was her round, she waited until I served her and yanked my head down to her level and said, 'I'm discrete and pure filth.'

One daring barrel of a woman came behind the bar and grabbed Sam's crotch and we had to lift her off her feet to remove her. She gained instant celebrity status and began stripping off.

Not long after we called last orders, two uniformed policeman came in. They had a word with Brian, then started ripping the Flash posters down. BOOOOOOOS echoed round and on their way out their helmets were whipped off and every missed lunge to retrieve them was followed by a WEHAAAY!

More black uniforms piled through the door and they began making arrests. A tall skinny lad wearing a Burberry baseball cap refused to go and held onto the fruit machine. They prised him off but his girlfriend grabbed his hand and dug her heels into a side partition and hung on, and on, then suddenly catapulted herself over her boyfriend and onto the copper and gouged at his face. The copper was squealing and the lad broke free as his girlfriend was wrestled to the floor. He waded straight back in and the whole place went up. Within seconds, just about every black uniform had a woman with a stiletto in her hand hanging off his back. A bar stool smashed off the optics behind me and I ducked down and crawled out the back door.

Sam and I went out the side doors and walked up the back lane, stopping short of the corner as two lads came towards us fighting. The smaller of the lads was swinging wildly and trying to ram his head into the other lad's stomach. They came together against the wall and the taller lad punched down on the other lad's head and back. The smaller lad dropped to his knees and Sam stepped in.

'Whoa! Whoa! He's had enough!'

The taller lad stepped back, arms open. 'Fuck off. Now.'

Sam: 'Like I said, he's had enough.'

The lad reached into his pocket and brought out his police badge.

Sam slapped it out of his hand and stepped up close. 'He's had enough.'

The lad picked his badge up and walked backwards, pointing at Sam.

I helped the smaller lad off the ground. His face was covered in blood and his shirt was ripped up the back, exposing red and purple scrapes on his white skin. His elbows and knuckles were badly scuffed and he could hardly stand up. I asked him if he needed an ambulance and he mumbled, 'Never seen him coming, never seen him coming', then staggered off down the lane.

A group of lads, who all seemed to be wearing white shirts splattered with blood, were into it just along from us. Five on five it looked, with two rolling around the floor and the rest running at each other then backing off. The two on the floor got up and wrestled standing up, throwing the head and knees in, they bounced off the phone box and fell through the café window.

The furniture shop on the corner had been ransacked and a mattress pulled out onto the street and set alight. Cars parked down neighbouring alleyways had been run over like toys.

The last of the men and women – kicking, screaming and spitting – were dragged into the police vans.

Through the broken front window of the Fiddler's we could see Brian, standing alone in the middle of the bar, hands clasped together and resting on his stomach.

11

Saturday Lunchtime.

The bar was empty, save for the old-timers and two
bouncers sat on stools at the front door. I was sat at the
end of the bar, head in hands, reading the early edition
of the Evening Chronicle. Tony Horn, the Metro Radio
morning DJ, had written, 'After the Faccome Flash's
appearance on Friday's show the phone lines were
jammed with well-wishers for his forth coming charity
streak at St James' Park. The Flash was as
accommodating off air as he was on, a real down-to-
earth lad, who has found himself a hero of the people
and who is prepared to go for it one last time to raise
money for his chosen charity. The debate on whether he
should be doing this is gathering momentum and local
MP, Alistair Fisher, called the show to urge people not
to encourage someone to break the law, even for
charity. I have a very strong opinion on charity and
believe you should hire the best people to make the
most money. Gone are the days of tin shaking. Charity
is big business and in this case, the Faccome Flash has
considerably raised the profile of Christopher

Sellhurst's condition and by the end of Friday's show there had even been offers of corporate sponsorship. It's not for me to say whether it's legal or not to support The Faccome Flash, but what I would say is that on the 17th March 2001, Billy Connolly kept his promise for comic relief and streaked naked around the statue of Eros in Piccadilly Circus. A group of over 50 men, sporting Connelly wigs, danced a highland fling in the nude not long after and all this was shown on BBC television.'

Earlier, the Northumbria Police Chief Constable had been interviewed on TV and had condemned last night's violence and said that the streaker had committed offences beyond the laws he had already broken himself, by inciting criminal activity. The reporter questioned the police's timing in removing the posters from the pub walls and their heavy-handed tactics afterwards. She suggested that the police had been insulted by the content of the posters and had taken it upon themselves to flex their authority in retaliation. The Chief Constable reiterated that it was the duty of every police officer to stop anyone breaking the law or encouraging criminal activity, which the posters clearly did. He rambled on about the fine relationship the coastal towns had enjoyed with the police and compared it with the town this morning, which was 'extremely tense and requires a strong police presence to ensure public safety'. After several pledges had been made to advertise on the Flash's body, he warned local media and businesses about their involvement in supporting an illegal event and that fines imposed would be aimed at deterring any similar events in the future and that the police would be doing all they could to arrest the streaker before Saturday.

Another part-timer came in at one o'clock and I was out the door before Brian could lay another guilt-trip on me and get me in front of those books.

I made my way through the crowds and into the barbers.

After my haircut, I went into Next and tried a few shirts on and chose a long-sleeved pinstripe with a white collar and cuffs, similar to the Paul Smith range that was out, but a quarter of the price. I also bought a pair of black boxer shorts, similar to the Calvin Klein ones that grip your thigh. When I got in, I put the heating on, lit the oil burner and downed a glass of warm milk and crashed out on the sofa.

*

'You've got be kidding me.'

I sat up and pulled myself together. 'What you on about?'

'That shirt,' Sam said, passing me a can of lager. 'Are you blind, or what? If there's anything going to stop you getting your leg over tomorrow, that shirt's it.'

'Bollocks.'

'Did you not see how many were wearing them last

night in the bar?'

'Not that many.'

'Not that many? It was like a vicar's convention, due to the fact... oh, hold on,' he said, checking in the bag, 'you've even went for the snide one from Next. Classy.'

'I'm on a budget, and tomorrow's going to cost a bomb as it is. I'm telling you now, I'll buy the first round, then it's Dutch after that.' Sam was shaking his head at me. 'I'm on a budget. I've had to sub of Brian as it is and I still haven't got any decent jeans, apart from -'

'Not those worn-out Diesel?'

'Those worn-out Diesel.'

'When I said you were guaranteed a ride, I meant with a little effort.'

'This is why I can't be arsed with a steady bird, the costs are ridiculous.'

'You're ridiculous and I hope you're not taking a lend of Brian.'

'He still owes me – AND – I've got Monday and Tuesday full days to do.'

Sam peeked into the bag and brought out my boxers. 'How is she going to resist you?'

'Unlike you, I don't need all the gadgets, natural charm sees me through.'

'Are you taking a pocket calculator to reckon up after each round, or are you going to rely on mental arithmetic?'

There was a knock at the door.

Sam answered and said, 'Cheers, Franky. No probs, mate, I'll drop it along tomorrow morning. You're a pal, cheers, okay, no probs, tomorrow, then, bye, bye.' Sam eventually shut the door and handed me the DVD player. 'You set it up and I'll get the vodka and fan mail.'

12

Sunday Night

The Grapes is slightly more upmarket than the Fiddler's and was at half capacity when Becky and Eve arrived, twenty minutes late, followed by another one of my shirts, taking the count to four. I turned away and ordered another vodka-tonic.

Sam went over to greet them and I checked Becky out through the mirror. She was even smaller than I remembered, with a blonde bob, cut short at the back in an inverted V, making her neck look long and thin. She was wearing black criss-cross tights, a green tartan mini-skirt and a black sparkly short-sleeved top that gathered at the shoulders and low down at the back and – she was giving me the finger back through the mirror. I waved and she made her way over.

'How's you?' she said.

I leant down and kissed her on the cheek.

'Not bad, you?'

'Sound, sound. Get me a voddy and Red Bull and one for Evey. Eve!'

'You're looking well,' I said.

'You what?'

I leant right down and repeated myself.

'Thanks. Like y'shirt,' she said, and pursed her lips.

'Ha, ha.'

Becky linked my arm and we moved away from the bar and sat in a booth at the front window and started chatting about the last time we had seen each other at the Christmas do. She pretended to be mortified that we'd ended up in the doorway and we both blamed the peach schnapps for the day-after amnesia.

She sunk her first treble vodka in three gulps, then started on Eve's, 'as she looks a bit busy'. After a long tale about Eve's ex, a psychotic, text-pest anorak, still in love with her, I went to the bar. When I returned, Becky was at the pool table, expertly chalking her cue.

'You any good?' I asked.

'Might be.'

We started playing and after only two visits to the table she was on the black.

'Loser gets the drinks,' she said, settling down to her shot.

'On the next game, make this a warm-up.'

She rested her cue against the table. 'I forgot, you're a right skintflint, aren't you?'

'I'm on a budget.'

She came round the table. 'What was it you were telling me last time?'

'About the writing?'

'Yeah,' she said, 'something about buying time until you found your inner something or other.' She beckoned me down to her level and gently touched my face, then pounced on me, shooting her tongue into my mouth and clasping her legs around my waist, forcing me back against the chalkboard.

As suddenly as she started, she broke off, still biting my lip.

'Ok, tight-wad,' she said, picking the cue back up. 'I pot this, you pay.'

As she was about to play her shot, I nipped her backside and she missed.

I had an easy red into the middle, then the black over the pocket.

I chalked the cue and sauntered round the table, checking the angles, eventually stretching over the green cloth, ready to take the shot. Becky stood alongside me with her back to the table. Casual as you like, she slipped her right arm underneath the cue and around my waist, leaned over my back, and with her left hand, started vigorously rubbing and squeezing my balls, like she was milking a cow. I spun around and she straddled me across the pool table and began devouring my face.

Two lads looking for a game interrupted the mauling and I lowered Becky to the floor.

She quickly led me through the bar and out into the rain.

'What's up?' I asked.

She flagged a taxi over. 'We're going back to yours.'

Armed with a half empty bottle of peach schnapps, we

fell through the flat door and into my room. Becky shoved me onto the bed and pulled my jeans off by the ankles, then whipped her top and bra off, while wriggling out of her skirt. She finished stripping and jumped on top and was soon in her stride, violently bucking forwards and groaning, totally oblivious to me as she went for it.

… As she was finishing, she pressed down hard with the heel of her left palm in the centre of my stomach; steadied herself on the wall with her right hand and slowed right down: long, deliberate, arched moves, each finished with a deep, *Aaaahhh*. Finally, she let out a prolonged moan and slowly dug her nails into my stomach until she was rigid – held it, slapped me across the face, then collapsed onto my chest.

We lay there for ages, giggling, messing with each other's hair, downing peach schnapps, Becky biting my neck and shoulders, Becky slapping me when my hand slipped below, Becky momentarily going down on me, Becky squeezing me tight and sobbing, Becky falling asleep in her tears. Becky catching me trying to finish myself off…

*

'Got any dope?' she asked, leaning up on my chest.

I stretched and interlocked my fingers behind my head. 'Never touch the stuff.'

'You're joking. I thought you'd be bang into it.'

'Can't see the point in it. Well, I can, you get stoned,

and if you've got problems and want to be out of it, fair enough. But it's just a temporary measure. Soon as it wears off, your mind goes back to the same place. That's why tapping into your unconscious mind is so good, you get long-term results.'

'How come?'

'Well, it depends how far you get into it, but basically, by tapping into your unconscious you find out more about yourself than your waking mind knows. So the decisions you make better suit the real you, and not the you who you think you are, if you know what I mean?'

'Mmmmm. Example.'

'Okay. Say you had a problem with someone at work and you were dreaming about them. Analysing your dream is a way of finding out what's really troubling you about them, and it might not be what you think.'

'Too complicated.'

'How so?'

'It just is. Why go to all that bother when you could just go over and have it out with them? Get it sorted there and then.'

'What if having it out with them isn't the solution?'

'How can it not be?'

'What if you have it out with them and afterwards still feel shitty? The reason why you're pissed off could be down to loads of things.'

'Too complicated.'

'Ever heard the saying, "sleep on it"?'

'Yeah.'

'Ever tried it?'

'Yeah.'

'Ever worked?'

'What do you mean?'

'When you've slept on a problem, have you ever come up with an answer that seemed impossible the day before?'

'Mmmm, can't remember, although I did consider murdering my ex most nights, but didn't.'

'Exactly.'

'That's got nothing to do with my subconscious. That's because the bastard came in so late I'd fallen asleep.'

'When your conscious mind is contemplating doing something out of character, like murdering your ex, your unconscious mind works at restoring the balance, so when you wake up you feel like giving him a good hiding rather than killing him.'

'Mmm.'

'You know when your mother says "I know you better than you know yourself?"'

'Boooring.'

'By tapping into your unconscious -'

'Got any tabs?'

I sighed.

'Yeah, we'll have to go in the front room to have one, though.'

Becky walked out butt-naked and stood in front of the Flash poster.

I stood next to her and gave her a cigarette and we

lit up.

'Any idea who it is?'

I shook my head.

'It's not you.'

'Cheers.'

'It's true, though, have you not seen the phone video?'

I declined her offer to watch it and went over to the window.

Sam had left the heating on and it was sweltering.

Becky shuffled in front of me and we both leant out the window and I got deja vu.

The streetlights were a mixture of yellow and white spreading as far as you could see, broken up by brilliant-white strips of motorway.

'Fancy something to eat?' Becky said. 'I'm starving.'

'Yeah, what do you want? I think we've got some chips and battered cod.'

She scrunched her face up and walked over to the phone and rang Domino's. I watched her as she went through the menu: cluster of freckles on her neck below the inverted V, narrow bony shoulders and tiny backside, red from leaning against me at the window. She finished ordering and I snaffled a bottle of Sam's vodka and we turned the lights off and flicked the hi-fi on.

The phone ringing interrupted us.

We both got up and I answered it – pizza man at the bottom of the stairs.

Becky grabbed the phone. 'Can you bring it up please? I can't, no, you'll have to bring it up, 805. No, I can't. I'm naked, I've just been having sex, thanks.'

She leapt into my arms and I swung her round and round and we fell onto the floor and went right at it again.

The doorbell rang and I prised her hands from around my neck and dropped her onto the sofa. I put my dressing gown on and answered the door. I paid the young delivery lad and closed the door. Becky opened it and gave him a full frontal, followed by a sultry wave.

After the pizza and a few more vodkas, we started to get really pissed again and Becky asked me if I believed in love at first sight. I said I did, then without thinking I said, 'But we've met before, haven't we?' She didn't reply, then marched into my room and got dressed. I followed her in and pulled my jeans on. Before I had a chance to get my shirt on, she had me across the bed, pulling my hair and biting my shoulders. She pushed me onto the floor and with a vodka bottle in one hand, sat astride me again...

I gave her my parka and I took Sam's denim jacket and beanie and walked her to the bus stop.

The bus took a while, in which time Becky became starving again and *needed* a kebab. We walked into town and she paid for two doners and a chips between us. We stood at the bus stop, watching the drunks bouncing off the shop shutters and staggering into doorways with their flies undone. Becky looked like one of the kids off The Lion The Witch and The Wardrobe in the parka. She turned around, cradling the kebab. 'So,' she said, 'you want to see me again?'

I bent down and kissed her. 'Course I do.'

She closed the kebab tray and tucked it under her arm and took out her mobile. 'Give me your number.'

'I haven't got a mobile.'

She stared at me.

'Seriously, I haven't got one. I can give you the flat number.'

She hurled the kebab in my face. 'Fuck off, liar!'

I stood there; head hanging limp, arms by my side.

I carefully scooped the sauce and lettuce from my eyes.

The bus pulled up and she got on.

She sat at the window staring straight ahead and gave me the finger as she passed.

I finished brushing myself down and made for the flat.

Halfway up the bank I saw Sam, heading along the path next to the railway line. He was on his own, shoulders hunched, hands in pockets and head down against the drizzle. I started after him. The lights were out in the park and I broke into a jog until I had passed through and made it up the embankment and onto the footpath. Sam was out of sight now, but I knew where he was headed.

Further along, the tarmac path had fallen away and I had to grab the wooden spiked fence to steady myself going round the corner. I stuck to the fence line all the way down to the allotments, then cut across the football fields and out onto Denham Ave. I pulled the collar up on my jacket and made for the cemetery gates.

The stone chapel and crematorium buildings were lit up, casting light on the first few rows of gravestones. I climbed over the fence and walked up the footpath and into the dark.

Sam was sat on a bench facing his father's grave. His pin-striped shirt was soaked to his skin. I sat in the shadows out of sight.

I remember when Sam's father used to come home after being away for days. You'd hear the commotion as he tried to negotiate his way along the back fences, mortal drunk. He'd fall into the long grass or shadow-box a tree or take a piss where he stood. One day, he took the short cut over the hill and rolled down it so fast that when he hit the bottom, he went into a forward flip and cleared our fence and landed face down on the lawn. *Thud!* Sam's mother was stood at the back door, chain smoking. I was at the bathroom window and could only see the toe of one of her slippers on the step and her right hand holding the cigarette.

An hour later, Sam's dad slowly got to his feet, staggered sideways and fell into the rose bushes, cutting his face and hands. He got up again, this time with more purpose, only to rip a sleeve from his suit jacket and tear his pants. Sitting awkwardly on the grass, he pointed up at me and shouted something. My mother suddenly opened the door and went to help him up.

'Leave him.' I felt sick when I heard Sam's mother's voice. I closed the window and never watched him come home again.

I took a slow walk up and sat next to Sam. I pulled a crushed box of cigarettes from my inside pocket and lit us both one.

We sat quiet, smoking.

Time passed.

Sam turned and looked at me, then looked away.

He looked at me again.

'What?'

He pulled a ring of onion off my hat, examined me further, then tilted my chin up and moved my shirt collar to one side. 'What the hell happened to you?'

I shook my head and started walking.

'Come on, then,' Sam said. 'Did you get her back or what?'

'I'm telling you, she's a proper psycho, her.'

We scaled the fence and started jogging back.

13

Monday afternoon.

Brian pulled his waistcoat tight, stepped forward, and dabbed at the till screen, ringing in a single gin. I cleared it. Shoulders back, he straightened the waistcoat and prodded the wrong button again.

'How the hell can you not see that green button?'

'I just can't.'

'Are you colour blind?'

He shook his head.

'Well what, then? Surely you can see with *them* glasses.'

He shook his head again.

'You can't see with your own glasses?'

'They're just for reading, really.'

'So where are your normal glasses?'

He looked at the floor.

I sighed.

'Why don't you get an eye test, Brian? And get some new specs.'

'I've got proper glasses.'

'So where are they, then?'

'She's got them.'

'She?'

'My ex-wife. These are hers.'

He shrugged. The glasses were staying and he wasn't going to be opening the till – well, not intentionally. So his presentation went like this: into the office where he'd show them the up-to-date books, *oh yes, keep on top of the paperwork and the place nearly runs itself*, then through to the lounge where he'd casually point out the poster for Thursday's Flash Karaoke Night, *the Flash is giving us his costume after Saturday, the knows* – points above the bar – *pride of place*, and also tells them his plans to increase revenue after Saturday's streak which included Flash merchandise, mats, pint glasses etc., regular fund raising nights for the Christopher Sellhurst Charity, and cheap beer for daytime drinkers, *10p off a pint means the world to a pensioner, the knows*.

The phone rang and Brian answered it. He handed it to me.

'Hello.'

'It's me.'

I paused. 'You alright?'

'So, so. Look, I just want to drop your coat off. You in later, or are you at work?'

'I'm not working but you can drop it at either, or give it to Sam.'

Long pause.

'I haven't got it at work.'

'Well, drop it round, if you don't mind.'

'Be after five.'

'No probs.'

'See you then.'

'See you then.'

Brian lifted his eyebrows.

'You don't want to know.'

'Sam said you were going steady, like.'

'You what?'

He nodded. 'Aye, told me this morning when he rang in about the mail. Said you said she could be the one.'

'Just for that, you can finish off in here yourself.'

I got my jacket and came from behind the bar.

One of the old-timers was waiting to be served. 'Hear you're going steady, Al. 'Bout time, kid, you're not as young as you were.'

When I got back to the flat, I went through the last few days of the dream journal and picked out the reoccurring elements. The hospital, Sam, Jack Nicholson, Tommy, Becky and I'm sure the gold and silver thing in a bag was a goldfish. I looked up goldfish. In Buddhism, the golden fish is the symbol of enlightenment. English dictionary, enlightenment – give information to. The goldfish had been in every dream since Sam had started streaking and fucked up my whole dream pattern. I lay back on the sofa, massaging my eyes, thinking only of the goldfish.

*

The phone ringing woke me.

I got up and answered it. 'Yeah?'

'Hi, it's me.'

'You alright?'

'Just wondering if you fancied a Chinese, my treat.'

'Eh, yeah, yeah. What time is it?'

'Six o'clock. You okay? You sound funny.'

'Yeah, yeah, sound, definitely, a Chinese, yeah.'

'Is Sam in?'

'Eh, no, I don't think so.'

'Okay, see you in about twenty mins.'

'See you then.'

I dived in the shower and brushed my teeth.

I went down and met Becky at the door.

She set the Chinese down and flung her arms around me.

I kissed the top of her head and we went upstairs.

'After you,' I said, showing her in.

She walked in and gasped, dropping the Chinese on the floor.

I followed her in.

Sam was standing in the middle of the living room in black underpants and a black mask with black and white tassels hanging down to his shoulders.

Time stood still.

I closed the door.

Sam strutted over to us, nodded, and went into his room.

Becky, hand still over her mouth, bimbled over to the

sofa and sat down. Knees tight together, she stared at the floor.

She suddenly jumped up. 'Is it really him? Is he really The Flash? Is Sam the Flash? Al? Is he really? I mean properly?'

Sam came out in his running gear, waved, and went out the door.

'He's the one,' I said, en route to the kitchen.

'I can't believe it. I physically can't take in that the bloke that walks past me every day is the Flash. Are you having me on? Is he really, Al? I mean the real Flash? On the radio and everything?'

I nodded.

'I can't believe it. I really can't. I mean he's properly famous and, well, you know, down there. I mean, all this time at work and he was walking about right in front of us and we never knew. Honestly, Al? You're not having me on?'

I came out with the two plates piled high and Becky followed me to the sofa.

'You just don't know the minute. It's true, you just don't know a person, do you? Who would have thought Sam the printer was The Flash. Yards away from us at work every day, and blessed with, well, you know.'

I nodded.

'Christ if the girls knew. If they KNEW! He'd have been mobbed the first day. And Josey, my mother's mate – she's a bit of a one, puts it about a bit – what she would do for him I couldn't repeat.' She took in a mouthful of food. 'Looking at the phone video, you'd never have guessed. No way, physically you'd never have guessed, probably because you're too busy looking at his, you know.

'Who would have thought, Sam, built like that, working feet away from me and Evey. Evey! The lucky so and so and she knocked him back! Can you believe it? If she had known, there's no *way* she'd have knocked him back. I mean, is there anybody, being realistic, who could?'

I put my fork down. 'Feel free to go in his room and wait. He'll be about, oooh what, forty minutes, make yourself comfortable. I'm sure he'd be delighted to oblige.'

She stared at me. 'Excuse me?'

'Well, could you resist? "Being realistic is there anybody who could?".'

She bounced her plate off my forehead, covering me in hot Chinese.

We both jumped up.

'You bastard! You think I'm that easy! Fuck you!'

She marched to the door. 'You'll never see me again!'

I ran out onto the landing and shouted down the stairs. 'And don't come back!'

She ran back up the stairs and I backed into the doorway.

'You know your fucking trouble! You don't know a good thing when it's happening to you! Well, you've blown it! It's over!'

She ran down the stairs.

I slammed the door and went inside to clean the maniac's mess up.

I was on my hands and knees scraping rice onto a plate when Sam arrived back.

He stood over me, trying not to laugh. 'What is it with you, her and food?'

I pushed past him and scraped the rice into the bin. 'She's officially banned from here *and* The Fiddler's. She's psychotic. By rights I should call the mental health department and have her sectioned.'

Sam took a shower and came back in with a couple of vodkas.

We sat on our sofas.

I lit up and gave him a couple off.

Sam said, 'Do you not think that it's just passion between you boiling over?'

'I've only been out with her for a total of about five hours and she's swilled me twice.'

'You did say she was a tremendous ride.'

'At what cost, though? She'll stab me next time.'

'I think you've fallen for her and you can't handle it.'

'Yeah, right.'

Sam walked over to the window. 'Al, you'll have to go down, she's still at the bus stop.'

'It'll only make it worse the more encouragement she gets.'

Sam steered me out onto the landing and handed me my parka.

I walked down the stairs.

As I opened the front door the bus pulled up.

I went back upstairs.

'Probably for the best,' I said, picking my glass up.

'You could always ring her.'

'It'll never work between me and her. She's divorced, hung up, looking for commitment. Me -'

'Shit scared to do anything unless you've managed to suss out every eventuality.'

'What you fail to understand is that I know the real me.'

'Life'll pass you by if you don't take chances.'

'Is that right? Before all this, who was bricking it to leave work and go travelling?'

'No, I wasn't.'

'Aye, you were. Worried about this, worried about that.'

'So how come I'm streaking in front of 52, 000 on Saturday if I haven't got bottle?'

'Never said you didn't have bottle. All I'm saying is that not buying into conventional life like me, is taking a bigger risk than having a rock steady career like you. I want to travel the world, see how others live. For all I know, there could be a much better life elsewhere that I could be living. You only get one shot, Sam. Travelling broadens your horizons, adding to your psyche, which up until sixteen has been moulded for you.'

'Don't start.'

'True, though.'

'I'd go travelling tomorrow.'

'Yeah, right.'

'After Saturday. No matter what, we're away.'

'Yeah, right.'

He stuck his hand out and I half-heartedly shook it.

'After Saturday, then.'

'After Saturday.'

14

Tuesday Morning

I sat up in bed, panting and sweating and tried to piece the dream together.

I was streaking across the pitch and Sam was chasing me, then we were in the flat and Sam was sat on his sofa in black underpants and the gimp mask trying to unzip the mouth. I got up to get a drink and noticed there was another door next to the kitchen, light coming from beneath it. I opened it and went in. I'm not sure what was behind the door, but I ended up walking down a hospital corridor with Sam, then I was in a wheelchair and he was pushing me.

We went into one of the rooms and Becky, dressed in a nurse's uniform, white sussies and heels, was whipping someone's bare backside. It was Sam and his head was turned to the side and he was laughing hysterically after every lash.

… Back in the flat, I stood and looked at the two extra doors between the kitchen and my room, both of which matched the other doors in the flat, down to the flaking paint. I opened the second new door and stepped into the cold and immediately recognised our garage from the old house where we'd had the fire. I walked around, rubbing my arms trying to keep warm. Sat in the corner, pulling hypodermic needles out of boxes and lining them up on the floor, were Sam and Jack Nicholson. The door leading into the house suddenly opened and my friend's mother from the bar, the one that claimed to be pure filth, poked her head in and said something to them and they got up and went through the door. Back at the flat, I was sat on my sofa with Becky, who was still in her nurse's outfit and Sam and Jack were on the other sofa, their bare legs entwined like they were an item.

I'm dreaming of Sam because I admire him and would like to have the bottle he has. The only hole in that theory is that he's always chasing me in the dreams, which indicates we have a similar quality. I have a completely different outlook on life to him and I couldn't do this streaking under any circumstances – life or death, no way. So what quality do we share and why is my subconscious so determined that I should realise what it is?

Jack Nicholson got into my dreams after I watched *One Flew Over The Cuckoo's Nest* the other night. What's worrying is that he hasn't left and it's been over a week. I've dreamt of movie stars before, the last one I think was Kate Winslet after watching Titanic. Two days max and she was gone. Jack Nicholson's been in every dream and the only help I can get from the dream book is that I aspire to be like him.

I tossed and turned and eventually got up and went and made a coffee. After a smoke at the window I settled in front of the TV just as the phone rang. I answered it.

'Hello.'

'Stick Radio One on! I'm on Chris Moyles in five minutes!'

'YOU-ARE-TAKING-THE-PISS!'

'I've already spoken to him! Bang a tape in and record it!'

I dived in front of the hi-fi and swept the videotapes and cassettes onto the floor, rummaged through them and stuck a tape in.

"CHRIS MOYLES SHOW: INTERNATIONAL RADIO 1..."

Chris Moyles: On the line we have the one and only The Faccome Flash!

Studio screamed and clapped.

- Flash my man! How are you, mate?

- I'm well, Chris, yourself?

A woman screamed and whistled.

- P-lease. You don't even know if it's true yet.

- Oh, it's true, Chris.

Studio went up again.

- Right... will you... will you... QUIETEN DOWN! Jesus, you're like a pack of sex- starved.... starved whatever! Jesus. Right, Flash. Me and you are similar, ahem, in many ways... we are! We both love footy, support crap teams and let's just say nature has been good to us.

- Certainly has, Chris, we're lucky boys.

Studio went crazy again, whooping and screaming and stamping their feet.

- Flash, I wanted you on the show on Friday when the story broke, mate, but as you know not everyone is backing you on this charity, ahem, 'walk'. The authorities want you off the streets... BOOOOOO...saying... BOOOOO... saying you're giving out the wrong message, you could be a paedophile for all they know, blah, blah. What do you make of it all?

Long pause.

- Chris, this started out as a laugh and still is to me, except Saturday will be for a good cause. Just about everyone I've seen or heard about are 100% behind me. The only reason the authorities aren't happy about it is that they can't catch me.

- Flash, you're already a hero up north and down here with us, but how would things change if you got caught? And would it not be a good thing, mate? You'd be in huge demand, who knows where it might lead?

- Chris, I'm more man than any of these coppers. They've tried, mate, they can't catch me.

- Yeah, but let's be honest. St James' Park, full capacity, and they know you're coming? Come on, you're not getting out of there, are you?

Long pause.

- You certain?

- Don't get me wrong I want you to escape, all I'm saying is Faccome's ground and Darlington's are nowhere near the security of Newcastle's and it's a HUGE, HUGE game against Man U. You'll be lucky to get in, never mind get out.

- How much then?

- For what? I'll donate, obviously, but I can't...'

- The bidding to advertise on my calves is up to five grand. What say you beat that and only pay if I get out?

Whooping and chants of 'go Flash, go' from the girls.

- Mate, if you get out of there I'll pay *FIFTEEN GRAND* to have the show on your calfs.

- You're on.

The studio went crazy and nothing Chris Moyles said could calm them.

Eventually.

- Flash, I wish you all the luck, mate.

- You're a star, Chris.

- Hey, us big fellers have to stick together! It's a pitty you couldn't somehow come see us at the roadshow tomorrow in Whitley Bay. Christ, it must only be ten or twenty miles from you, is it?

- About that.

- Under a vale of secrecy, protected by the Morning Breakfast Crew. Anything's possible, mate.

Silence.

- What do you say, Flash? There'll be a hell of a crowd and over seven million listeners? Chance to raise more money for Christopher Sellhurst.

Long pause.

- Anything's possible, Chris.

- So you'll come and us big fellers can hang out together – NOT LITERALLY!

By the time the studio had quietened down, Sam had gone.

I stubbed my smoke out, ran into my room and speed dressed; into Sam's room, pulled his jeans over mine and his t-shirt, grabbed my parka and ran out the door.

By the time the bus pulled into the concourse at Newcastle, I was soaked in sweat and itching like mad between the legs to the point where I nearly ripped the jeans off and flung them down the aisle. I was first off the bus and marched up onto Percy Street and stood on the corner, opposite the Three Bulls, letting the drizzle and breeze cool my face.

I took a slow walk up to St James' Park.

As I reached the start of China Town, the stadium came into view perched on a bank overlooking the town. A magnificent, state-of-the-art colosseum, with long, tinted windows beneath silver stanchions. I leant back against the window of the all-you-can-eat Chinese restaurant and watched everyone going about their business.

A couple of doors down, Fluid Bar were advertising Saturday's match and would be the perfect spot to hide Sam's clothes. We had agreed on the Strawberry, but standing here, it looked too close to the stadium.

I crossed the road, through the car park and up the stairs to the Newcastle Brown Ale stand. There were a few supporters outside the club shop and Shearer's Bar. I walked up the narrow lane towards the east stand.

Opposite the turnstiles, there were stone terraces, four storeys high, running the length of the stadium, and to the left, James Avenue, which took you down towards Percy Street. The first pub you'd come to that way was The Goose, which was too far.

I casually looked around, started the stopwatch and let rip, head down, arms pumping, fast as I could, eye on the Strawberry Pub, knees to chest, WHOOOOSH! Feet head height and SLAM! Flat on my back, rain peppering my tongue as I tried to breathe. I've never felt pain like it knifing my ribs as I struggled to take the smallest of breaths.

I was frightened to move: broken spine, fractured skull, slipped disk, cracked ribs.

I lifted an arm, a shoulder, then my head, before rolling over onto my front. I used the wall to get to my feet and held the small of my back, taking slow, short breaths, staring at the green skid mark on the cobbles.

One side of the alley was covered in moss, the other, shiny cobbles off the rain. We'd both need to take the outside on Saturday and hope for dry weather. I gingerly made my way down the street and into town.

In Waterstones, I picked up *Every Dream Interpreted* by Veronica Tonay PhD. PhD, I thought. I turned into a corner and began reading it. It was sensational. It gave so many more options on how to interpret dreams than the other book. I went to the index and looked up house dreams – distorted, famous houses, foundations, house of friends, people within, childhood homes and rooms. I flicked to p246. Along with water, houses are an agreed-upon symbol among psychologists. In dreams, houses represent layers of the psyche, a map of the dreamer's conscious and unconscious mind. What is in there? Is it unfamiliar or dark? The dreamer is dreaming about unconscious feelings and thoughts. Or is it familiar and sun-filled? This house contains mostly what the dreamer already knows about himself. Is it old? Not much change has happened. Or is it new? Transformations are afoot.

I flicked forward to 'discovering new rooms'. These dreams seem to occur when dreamers are discovering new things about themselves. Often the dreams are discovered with delight. Sometimes, they are frightening and unsettling, as dreamers face the unknown. If you have such a dream and get inside the new room, recall carefully what inhabited it. What was the furniture like? Was anyone inside? What does the physical appearance of the room suggest about a recently discovered part of you?

'Excuse me?'

I looked down at the assistant, who was about four foot. 'What's up?'

'Don't mind you browsing, sir, but this isn't a library.'

I handed him the book. 'I'll take it.'

'Very good.'

I followed him to the tills.

'That'll be £14.99, please.'

'How much? £14.99?'

He nodded.

I pulled the book out of the bag and checked the price: £14.99.

'Not on offer, then?'

He shook his head.

'No seconds?'

There wasn't.

I scraped together fourteen quid.

'Look, mate,' I said, leaning over the counter. 'Any chance you could let me off with the ninety-nine pence? To be honest, I wasn't expecting to find something so…' He was shaking his head with great pleasure.

'Fair enough,' I said, straightening up. 'I'll leave the fourteen quid and nip to the cash point. Be a couple of minutes.'

An hour later, a regular from the Fiddler's, all suited and booted for his office job, strolled past and I jumped off the monument steps in my parka with the hood up like a crazed wino and started blabbing on about losing my cash card and getting home. He slipped me a crisp twenty and I promised to sort him out next time he was in the bar.

I strode through the double doors into Waterstones

wafting the twenty around like I was struggling to keep it under control. The little git ignored me, but I stayed put and leant against the counter, looking away from him, the twenty between two fingers. With no one left to serve and nothing on the horizon, he took the note and rang it in. He dropped the change in the bag with the book and hooked it over my fingers and I walked out.

I sat outside Starbucks with a coffee and read the section on People We Don't Know. Famous people, same analysis as the other book, artists and writers, entertainers, politicians, strangers, scientists, sports heroes. Then I came to Dreaming Of Lunatics. Crazy people are relatively common in dreams. Most of us have had fears of going mad at one time or another, so the dream lunatic presents us with a picture of pure irrationality that can, at times, be oddly soothing. Being rational all the time can be exhausting. In its extreme form, the lunatic dream figure can represent a need to throw logic to the wind.

Jack – Cuckoos' Nest, The Shining. Becky – five hours, two swillings and lumps out of my shoulder and neck. Sam – The Facomme Flash. The definition was 'lunatic figure', so they didn't have to be fully fledged. But what about the house dreams? The goldfish? The hospital?

I'd like to think that after six months of analysing dreams, my subconscious has something more important to tell me other than 'throw logic to the wind'.

I went into Boots for some painkillers, then headed home.

15

Wednesday Morning

CHRIS MOYLES SUPPORTS THE FACCOME FLASH 0800 4564 6592, PLEASE GIVE GENEROUSLY... CHRIS MOYLES SUPPORTS THE FACCOME FLASH 0800...

Standing in the field punching the air and singing with the rest of the 5, 000 plus crowd, I looked down and Sam handed me his jeans and jumper. Soon as he stood up, hysteria swept through the crowd like a Mexican Wave and he struggled to get through to the stage where Chris Moyles was waiting, arms open. 'What did I tell you? What did I tell you? And here's my mate the one and only THE FACOMME FLASH!'

Sam looked every bit the super hero: black underpants, bare-chested, black and white tassles resting on his shoulders. Bras, knickers, t-shirts, skirts and a blow-up doll landed around him. The police moved in from both sides, trying to break the resistance of the crowd who had joined hands and were standing firm.

-You made it, Flash! What do you make of this crowd here for you? It's a roadshow record!

- I love them, Chris! They're the best!

The police were getting closer.

- You're not breaking any laws today, mate, so you can stay, yeah?

Sam edged away, the mic still in his hand.

- Would love to, but the boys in blue are itching to get a look under the mask, Chris, and as I've said, the only way they'll do that is if I let them.

- But, mate, there's nowhere to go. You're safe here with us. ISN'T HE?

The topless crowd had worked themselves into a frenzy as the police closed in on the stage.

I ducked under the barrier tape and sprinted for the corner of the field. I looked over my shoulder, expecting to see Sam giving it big licks, but a copper was on my tail. I bounced off the wall as I ran through the cut, looked both ways, then ran up the street and into the first garden that didn't have a garage.

Sam was legging it for the cut, where a copper was waiting, tight up against the wall. I pulled myself over the fence and ran towards him, waving his clothes above my head, SOS style. He spotted me and I took off back up the fence line. He soon caught up and we both hurdled a low fence and out into the front street.

A police car turned the corner and we ran back into the garden and started hedge- hopping. Three gardens up we stopped and listened. Sirens, doors slamming, shouting, radios out on the field. The back door of the next house along slowly opened and an old woman, carrying a small basket of washing, froze. She looked at Sam, me, back at Sam, then waved us over.

We went through the kitchen and into the front room, where she was closing the curtains. She put a finger to her lips and pointed to the sofa and armchair. We sat down and the old woman walked between us and patted Sam on the shoulder. She went out the front door and we could hear her talking to her neighbour about the Flash.

'I wish he'd knocked on my door, Edith, I would have dragged him in.'

'In our day he wouldn't have made it down the High Street, we'd have had his pants round his ankles.'

'Aye, Hin, man like that, and he's meant to be a good lad. Our Stacey knows someone that knows him, meant to be a lovely, lovely, lad. Good family and that.'

'So they say. And hung like a donkey. Some say bigger.'

'Aye, like a donkey.'

'Wouldn't mind a look.'

'Aye, I'd have a look, Hin, just to see.'

Sam had changed into his clothes and taken the mask off by the time the old woman came back in. 'Well, boys, they're still out there looking for you.'

Sam stood up and offered his hand. 'Thanks for taking us in, we were snookered there.'

She waved his hand away and stood at the fireplace. 'Most exciting thing that's happened on this block in ten years. Whole street's out there wishing they had you indoors. Mind,' she said, lighting a rolly, 'you've been blessed with the works, haven't you? Eh? We all thought you must be ugly, what with the mask. And who's this handsome lad?'

I offered my hand and she waved it away through the thick smoke. 'I'm Alex.'

'Edith. And you boys are welcome. I only wish our Nicola was here. You got a girl?' Sam shook his head. 'You'd love Nicola. Big, big chest, Nicola. But nice with it. Decent girl. You'd be proud to have her on your arm.' She passed a photo round of arguably the worst-looking girl in the northern hemisphere. 'See. I just wish she could find the right one. You want her number, Flash?'

'Actually, I'm not dating much until after Saturday.'

She shoved a piece of paper into his hand.

'If you were around when the war was on, I tell you something. When I was in my twenties, with the girls? You'd have loved us. You wouldn't have been able to get enough of us, I tell you. The Yanks loved us every day of the week and sometimes more when a ship docked. You'd have gone down a storm with a cock like that. It's a blessing, son. Take it from me and use it like it's going out of fashion. Any chance of a quick look, Flash? Just to see it up close, like?'

Sam, mouth hanging open, shook his head and Edith shuffled off into the kitchen to make a cup of tea.

I checked out the window but couldn't see as far as the cut.

Edith came in with the teas. 'There you go, boys. I've rang our Nicola, just to put her in the picture. She asked if you could leave your number, you know, in case she needs to get in touch.'

Sam jotted down something on the paper and gave it back to her.

I checked out the window again.

Edith picked up the phone and put her glasses on and dialed a number. 'Helen, it's Edith, number sixty-four. Yes, pet. Is your mother there? Jean, it's Edith. I have, I have. What I'm ringing for is that I've got him here with me. Aye,The Flash. What we need to know is, is there any police next to you? I'll hold, pet. There isn't. That'll do.'

Sam moved uncomfortably in his seat and I asked to have a look out the back. When I returned, Edith was on the phone to someone else asking for information on the police's whereabouts and letting them know that The Flash was safe and sound at number sixty-four. Sam and I stood up just as the doorbell sounded. We sat back down.

Edith answered the door and came back in with Jean, from down the street. Jean had a good look at Sam. 'Well, he is, isn't he? Aren't you, Flash?'

Edith winked at Sam and said, 'He might with an audience, that's his thing, isn't it?'

The doorbell rang again and another pensioner was

shown into the small living room. Sam asked to use the toilet and I followed him out into the passageway. From the living room, we heard Edith shout, 'And here's our Nicola!'

Sam opened the front door and the two of us ran and jumped the garden wall, staggered across the road and pelted down the street, laughing our heads off.

16

Thursday Night

Thanks to an alteration to the poster by one of the
punters, the Flash Karaoke Night had turned into the
Flash Fancy Dress Party and we were inundated with
pimps, hippies, Elvises, prostitutes and a furry shark,
who was sat at the end of the bar sweating buckets. The
best performance on the mic so far had come from one
of the old-timers who had sung Love Me Tender and,
unlike all before him, he'd kept his kit on.

Everyone was well pissed and things were getting
messy when Sam came through the doors as Freddy
Mercury in skin-tight white pants. I could see the bulge
from the bar, so it must have looked obscene up close
and he disappeared under a swarm of blonde curly wigs
and white arses.

He made his escape and arrived behind the bar, his
vest and tash hanging off. 'Jesus God, Al, they're
savages. Look.' Both front pockets of his jeans had
been ripped clean off and his thighs were bleeding.

I stuck his tash back on. 'If you throw the bait out,

you can't complain when you get a bite, can you?'

He poured himself a large vodka, downed it, and we joined in the chants as another completely naked woman well over forty was escorted off the premises by two officers.

It was after nine o'clock when I got a call from my mother.

'What's up,' I asked, lighting a cigarette.

'I've been trying to get hold of you all week. You haven't been down. Is everything okay?'

'Yeah, sound, it's just been manic in here every night with the streak getting closer. It'll be back to normal next week.'

'And I can't find Tommy anywhere. Have you seen him?'

'Never seen him all week. Have you tried the club.'

She had.

'His flat?'

'Neighbours said they haven't seen him coming or going all week. That's not to say he hasn't been. I know he had a good win last week, so he'll probably be enjoying himself. Which explains why he hasn't been round to see me.'

Brian kept opening the door.

'I wouldn't worry too much, he'll surface when he's ready. I'll go round tomorrow. Wake the lazy git up.'

'You don't think there's anything seriously wrong with him, do you? He hasn't said anything to you, has he? You know he tells me nothing, Alex, so I need you to be honest. He hasn't confided in you, has he?'

'How could he? I haven't seen him.'

'It's not like you two not to see each other for a week, is it?'

'It's only because I've been working days this week.'

'I suppose.'

'Look, I really have to go.'

'Oh, before I forget, I've cut a writing competition out of the paper for you. It's for non-published writers with a novel.'

'Sound, I'll get it off you tomorrow.'

'And you'll go round and see Tommy?'

'Like I said.'

'And you'll let me know what's what?'

'See you tomorrow.'

I hung up.

Brian opened the door again.

'I'm coming.'

He rolled his eyes.

'What?'

Becky was stood in the corner of the bar on her own. She was wearing a dogtooth coat with big lapels and a Doctor Who scarf. She had shopping bags over her arm and a big black leather handbag over her shoulder. I showed her through the side door and into Brian's office.

I sat on the corner of Brian's desk, arms folded.

Becky handed me a white carrier bag.

I frowned. 'For me?'

She nodded.

It was a Paul Smith shirt.

I stood up and wraped my arms around her.

After a while, she started crying.

'What's up?'

'Nothing, nothing. It's nothing.'

We started kissing and I lifted her up onto Brian's desk and ripped her knickers down and off at the feet and she frantically undid my jeans.

There was a knock at the door, then Brian stuck his head in. 'Al, you'll have to come out, we can't cope.'

'Can you give us five minutes?'

'They're trying to pull Sam over the counter and You-Know-Who is back in.'

'Come on,' Becky said, getting down off the desk. 'I'll give you a hand. I used to work in the Ship years ago. Come on.'

She steered Brian out and we piled along the corridor.

17

Friday Morning

Becky and I were sitting crossed-legged on the floor, going through the morning papers. All the tabloids had Sam and Chris Moyles on the front page and the story was that Moyles was going to be suspended for backing The Flash.

Moyles' guest this morning was the Northumbria Police Chief Constable, who was making a second appeal to the public to come forward if they knew The Flash's identity. After Moyles had reeled off a list of famous streakers that hadn't been charged, he accused the police of wanting to make an example of The Flash because he was making fools of them.

The Chief Constable said that this streaker was repeatedly breaking laws that could include indecent exposure, outraging public decency, breach of the peace and public nuisance. He also said that it could take years to get over copycat streakers or worse crimes incited by this streaker, because the story was getting so much publicity and the streaker was seen by many, including Moyles, as a hero.

Chris Moyles started getting lippy and the Chief Constable warned him about his own involvement, 'which we're looking at in great detail'. The interview finished with Moyles thanking the Chief Constable for his time then playing the Benny Hill theme tune.

The *This Morning* show were doing a report from outside the Fiddler's and they estimated that over £80,000 had been collected for the Christopher Sellhurst Charity and that a further £40,000 had been pledged by companies to advertise on the Flash's body. It all ended light heartedly with the female reporter rooting for the 'ultimate man'.

I switched the radio over to Metro and Tony Horn, who had campaigned for The Flash all week both on air and in his newspaper column, made the prediction that 'against all odds the North East's own super hero will escape and ride off into the sunset'.

Becky had lost it big-time and she was starting to freak me out with a never-ending list of dangers that we faced tomorrow, now that things had gone 'national'. National police strategy, national security, national coverage, national pile of shit in my pants if I listened a second longer.

I walked her to the bus stop.

When I got back to the flat, I decided not to watch any more TV or listen to the radio and I didn't phone Sam. God knows how he was keeping it together.

I got my coat and headed to Tommy's.

Tommy lived about a quarter of a mile from my mother's in three–high retirement flats called Albany Court. I took the long way round, avoiding my mother's and enjoying the fresh air and sunshine. I walked along the footpath adjacent to Albany Court and peered over the fence and Tommy's curtains were the only ones drawn.

The caretaker was sat outside, which meant the front door was unlocked. I jogged up the two flights of stairs to Tommy's flat and banged on his door. Again. And again.

Mr Allen at number seven came out. He was tiny and always wore a mustard cardigan and thick-rimmed square glasses. Tommy called him Corbett. He was my mother's spy and Tommy rapped on his door and shouted through his letterbox when he came in pissed, 'to give the nosy fucker something to grass about'.

'Not been in for days,' Mr Allen said, shaking his head. 'Must have eventually given him accommodation at the Lonely Heart's Club.'

I stuck my tongue out at him and walked away.

Outside, I walked over to the caretaker who shook his head as I approached. I gave him the finger and walked down the gravel drive and away.

After waiting two hours, I got to see Tommy's doctor. Doctor Black was old school and had been giving Tommy prescription painkillers and signing him off on the sick without any examination for years. Tommy used to send his wife up to collect his prescriptions and now he had conned my mother into doing it.

Doctor Black shrugged when I expressed our concerns for Tommy and I had to agree. What could anybody say to Tommy that would make him change his ways? One piece of good news was that he wasn't in hospital otherwise Black would have known about it.

I thought about breaking into his flat, but I knew the caretaker would have been in already. Tommy reckoned the caretaker made a fortune nicking the deceased's belongings before the family got there. Tommy reckoned everyone was making a fortune doing this or that.

I traced his route to my mother's, the club, the off-licence and the bookies. Nothing. The only other explanation I could think of, apart from him lying in some gutter, was that he had found some new pub to frequent with the influx of cash from his win.

Time was getting on so I made for the Fiddler's.

18

Friday Night

Brian had every member of staff, including Becky, crammed behind the bar, while he squeezed onto the seats next to the old-timers with his dishcloth and pint. The place was rocking as much, if not more, than last night and the police had doubled their presence inside and outside the bar.

Becky was doing my head in and I made my excuses and left before last orders. I stopped on the bank and sat on a bench and lit a cigarette.

I looked across the park at the footpath next to the railway line and pictured him tearing onto the pitch at Darlington, hand aloft, panting when he joined me in the bar, running through the streets laughing and collapsing onto the train platform.

The escape route wasn't any further than Darlington and the only extra security would be on the touchlines. Like Sam had said, there are only so many people that can stand in front of an exit door and every time we'd been to a decent match, there had only ever been one.

Take out the crowd, the fact it was Newcastle v Man

U, and the situation was the same as before. He could do it. I knew he could and I'd make it to Fluid Bar. Even if I slipped on the cobbles I'd be up, the adrenaline pumping. I'd make it because I had to. Because my best mate, sitting up at his father's grave, couldn't take being caught and shamed. I know he couldn't and now that it was here, he was digging deep, preparing himself, blocking out all this madness.

I waited until the last of the revellers had either been taken away by the police or had gone home. I smoked a cigarette, thought about going up to the grave to sit with him, thought better of it, then went back to the flat to wait.

19

Saturday Morning

The sound of the phone ringing woke me.

I rolled off the sofa and answered it.

It was Sam.

'Where are you?'

'Al, listen. I've been nicked.'

'Eh?'

'I've been nicked! I'm in Facomme police station now.'

'You what?'

'Get down here, this is the only call I've got.'

The line went dead.

I grabbed my jacket and ran out the door.

An officer showed me into Sam's cell and locked the door behind me.

Sam got up from his concrete bed and we hugged.

'Tell me it's not what I think it is,' I said.

He shook his head and shuffled around the tiny cell.

'I'll ring my cousin, Shaun. You know, the solicitor? But I need to know exactly what's been said. Do they know or what?'

He stood, hands outstretched, touching the pale wall. 'They know.'

I checked for cameras, then whispered, 'What evidence do they have? They can't lock you up for something you haven't done yet.'

'That's all they said when they nicked me at work.'

'At work!' I started pacing. 'That's not on. Shaun'll sort this. Soon as I ring him he'll get you out.'

Sam sat down, head in hands.

'Look, I'll have you out in an hour. He's got contacts. Judges, barristers, he knows everyone. They can't lock you up on a hunch.'

'They're not letting me out until after full-time.'

Keys rattled in the lock.

Sam looked up and said, 'Everything you need is under my bedside drawers, Al. You've got to do.'

'Don't be fucking ridiculous. How can I do it? How can I fucking do it? Think about it. Think about what you're saying. That's a non-starter and you know it. Let's think rationally, which is how we're going to get you out of here before kick-off.'

I barged through the crowds, getting pushed one way then the other. I made it to the phone box outside The Fiddler's and rang Shaun. He answered. I told him everything. In between gasps he said, 'Honestly, mate, if they've got him locked up that's exactly where he'll stay until after the final whistle. Tony Blair or the Queen couldn't even help, he's been taking the piss out of the law.'

I dropped the receiver and stared through the scratched and graffitied glass of the phone box at the bedlam before me. I pushed the door open and tunnelled my way through coats, scarves, screaming, balloons, chinking donation buckets, burgers, candy floss. I NEEDED AIRRRRRRRRRRRRRRRR!

I sat on the same bench as last night, taking long, deep breaths. I looked down at the sea of red and white, black and white, the camera crews, then dropped onto my hands and knees and retched. I couldn't do this. Couldn't do this, spew, couldn't do this, couldn't do this, spew, everything you need is under the drawers, spew, spew, spew...

I sat back up on the bench. I had time. What to do? What to do? I checked either side of me, then discreetly put my hand down the front of my jeans. It was smaller than it had ever been before. Minute. The size of a newborn child's. Smaller. I got the gushes again and started walking.

I was on my hands and knees in the bathroom when Becky arrived.

'Alex!' She helped me over to the sofa. 'Eve rang, not knowing that Sam was who he was, and told me that he'd been arrested at work and they all thought it was drugs because of all the designer shirts he wears, but I knew otherwise. What are we going to do? Will he be out in time? What if he's not? The sponsorship and everything. Al?'

I hung right out of the window, feet barely touching the ground.

Becky brought me a glass of water.

After I finished it, I let the glass slip out of my hands and watched it all the way down.

I wanted Becky to ramble on, tell me how impossible it was with what I was packing, but she just rubbed my back and cuddled into me.

20

'Okay,' I said, turning around. 'Super-fast super-well-hung Sam isn't doing the streak. He's banged up until after full-time. Guaranteed. No getting him out. Not happening. So you tell me where that leaves us, eh?'

Becky handed me a lit cigarette.

'He asked me to do it. How the hell can I do it? I can't make it out, so that means I'll get caught and get seen with what will be the smallest knob in history by the time I hit the turf.'

Becky handed me another glass of water.

'So here I am at the side of the pitch, mask on, tiny knob out and all the players and officials are rolling around laughing and then I try to make it out and the fun really starts. Fuck me, they'll have a field day. The only hope is that they catch me quick. Which defeats the object which gets me, back, to...' Becky had undone my jeans and went down on me, 'back to where we, errr... started. Which is, errr, that...'

'See!' she said, triumphantly standing back. 'You run on the pitch like that and you'll fool a few people.'

'I run out like this and I'll be locked up for life for being a paedophile.'

I leant back out of the window.

'I can't do this,' I said, coming back in.

'Course you can.'

'I won't be able to run on the pitch without spewing. I know I won't.'

'I'll help.'

'My life'll be ruined. I'll have to emigrate.'

'If you like, just before you put the mask on, I'll suck you off. It'll still be up by the time you run on the field.'

'Can you imagine the look on people's faces when you suddenly drop to your knees?'

'I'll do it, Al,' she said, putting her arms around me. 'Then all you need to worry about is getting out.'

The second I thought about the edge of the pitch, that moment, the bile rose up my throat. I physically couldn't do this.

I hung back out of the window.

It was sunny and cold.

Droves of Faccome FC supporters were heading for the train station, kids with balloons, mams in scarves and hats, dads singing, already pissed up, teenagers in Flash masks and grandmas and granddads in their Sunday best. Most of them didn't even have match tickets.

*

I took my t-shirt and jeans off, then my underpants and

walked over to Sam's sofa and pulled the folder out from under his cushion and handed it to Becky along with the marker pens. I stood in front of the mirror, hands spread-eagled on the wall. 'Start with my back and use the stencils to get the company logos as near as you can to what's on the sheet.'

21

I knelt in front of Sam's bedside drawers, reached under for the mask and jerked back when I felt something cold. Lying on my stomach, I got hold of the jeans and eased them out, then sat back on my honkers. The gimp mask wasn't the only thing he'd bought from the sex shop that day.

Using toilet paper, I picked the rubber dildo up and examined it. The base and balls had been hollowed out and elastic sewn around the edge. I went into the kitchen and pulled on rubber gloves and scrubbed the whole thing with disinfectant, rinsed it, then did the same again.

Back in Sam's room, I pulled a condom on, then the dildo and pranced around in front of his full-length mirror, shaking it this way and that, diving onto the bed, twisting and turning and pretending to take a piss. All this time! All this attention! The women! And not a word, even to me!

I walked back and forth, watching it slap against my thighs. What it would be like to have this for real? I spun around, jumped up and down. It never budged.

'How disappointing is that?' Becky said, standing in

the doorway.

I held it with one hand. 'Feel the weight of it. How real?'

'Not as good as the real thing, though, is it? And here's me looking at Sam, thinking…'

'Thinking what?'

Becky stared at me, then grinned. 'Are we going to make it out of there, or what?'

Wouldn't be so bad getting caught now. In fact, getting caught as long as King Rubber Dong stayed on would be a good thing. Even if it came off when they got hold of me, it would be their word against the 52,000 who had seen it first hand. I'd be on every newspaper, all the TV interviews, the man that no one could catch revealed to the world. Exposed and shamed and stepping into his best mate's shoes, that no one could ever fill. Jesus Christ, how the hell was I going to make it out of there?

I rang Tommy's number.

'Tommy?'

'Al?'

'Where you been?'

The phone went muffled.

'I've only hit the jackpot, haven't I?' he whispered.

'I heard you had a decent win.'

'Who told you that, like? Corbitt? The nosy fucker.'

'Tommy, I'm in bother.'

Long pause, big sniff.

'Bother?'

'Major.'

Long pause, big sniff.

'You still there?' I asked.

'Anyone we know?'

I told him I needed him to come straight to the flat and not to drink anything.

'I'll have to get shot of Lucy first.'

'Lucy?'

The phone went muffled again, then, 'That's where I've been all week. She's only forty-eight. Used to be a model,' big sniff. 'Been at her gaff all week, haven't I?'

'So where'd you meet her?'

'Errrm, can't remember.'

'You can't remember?'

'Ermmm, I think it was the, what's its name?'

'The club?'

It wasn't

'The Anchor?'

'Not the Anchor.'

So it had to be the bookies and he'd had a big win.

I told him to get straight to the flat.

After I had finished getting dressed, I stood at the window and had a smoke.

Becky shouted and I came back in and she handed me the phone.

'Hello.'

'I've got it.'

'Brian?'

'They gave me the job. I'm manager.'

'Well, I hope I'm in for a promotion! We'll have a right old knees-up after the big one today, eh?'

'I've already told the regulars it'll be a free bar for an hour, but just this once.'

'Fantastic. Fantastic. Count me in. Look, Brian, I need your help.'

'What do you need?'

'Can you leave the bar now and meet me outside the Strawberry in Newcastle?'

'Who's going to look after the bar?'

'I'm desperate. I'll explain when I see you.'

As I hung up, Tommy appeared at the door, huffing and puffing.

I turned him around. 'I'll explain on the way.'

22

Standing at the top of the stairs at the entrance to the Newcastle Brown Ale stand, I looked down across the car park and China Town and it was a mass of black and white shirts. There were police on horseback and in groups along the front of the stadium and on the corner next to the Strawberry. I kissed Becky off and went through the turnstile.

With five minutes to kick-off, supporters were still necking pints, stuffing pasties and sauage rolls down, placing bets at the Ladbrokes stands and watching highlights of Newcastle's famous 5 – 0 thrashing of Man U many seasons ago. I looked along the line of exits and there were two stewards on every door. I thought about having a swift half to calm my nerves, but I needed some air – and fast.

I made my way through to the lower-tier seats, found mine and picked a programme off the floor and tried to read the notes from the manager. The MC announced that Newcastle United were coming out and the crowd went crazy, waving scarves above their heads and chanting 'TOON TOON, BLACK AND WHITE

ARMY, TOON TOON, BLACK AND WHITE ARMY!'

I looked around the amazing stadium, packed out with black and white shirts, the pitch lush green, stewards and ball boys spaced out along the touchlines and police at the exits. I stared at the edge of the pitch, the way it curled up to the white line, how clear it was, how real. I sat down, taking slow breaths, nice and easy. If I passed out, I couldn't do it. And there was no question I was going to. That edge of grass, down there just right of the goal, was where I was going on, not now, not now, but soon, maybe after half-time. Hands on my thighs, off with the jeans, sweatshirt, mask on, down to the edge, over the white line, on the pitch, in play, doing it. Oh, Jesus God.

Manchester United were all over Newcastle and the home supporters had quietened down. After only thirty minutes, Newcastle made the substitution the crowd had been waiting to see all season. Newcastle United legend Alan Shearer was coming on. I stood up with everyone else and clapped, then sat down and gripped the jeans, deep breaths, deep breaths, deep breaths, nice and easy here we go, AHHHHHHHHHHH! The vomit shot out of my nose and mouth all over the people in front. I rushed along the row, apologising, hand over my mouth as more sick squirted out of the sides and onto people's laps.

A steward followed me into the toilets, then left when he realised I wasn't drunk.

I had a drink of water from the tap and stood in the middle of the toilets. The pale walls were the same colour as the cell Sam was in. I walked around in the sodden mess, lap after lap after lap, thinking of Sam on that concrete bed. You've got to do it, Al. Everything you need is under my bedside drawers. Not everything Sam. Not everything. Come on, come on, deeper breath, come on, you can do this, edge of the pitch, arms going, come on, come on.

I stopped plodging and lifted my head and stared at the light blue wall above the urinals. I saw straight through the wall, Sam urging me on, pointing at the pitch, Becky and Tommy waiting, screaming for me to make it. An old fellow came into the toilet and stood looking at me. I nodded at him and ripped off my top and handed it to him, then my jeans and t-shirt, pulled the mask on and ran out of the toilet, through the access and sprinted for the edge of the pitch.

As I hurdled the advertisement board, an almighty roar went up and I was off, running for my life...

Short sharp breaths – one two, one two, one two, heart hammering, eye on the centre of the pitch, come on!

Straightening up, I saw the crowd for the first time, screaming for me, punching the air, kids, dads, mams, going crazy. I reached the centre circle, stewards and police closing in like they were being sucked down a plug hole. I turned a full circle, arms aloft, and yelled, 'COME OOOOOOOOOON!'

The roar got louder and I got faster, swerving round one steward, then another, past two police, you're not fast enough mate, or you, or you, or you, or you, come on!

Past Ronaldo, more stewards, left, right, I'm flying, past Rooney, another steward, getting faster and stronger, taller, the crowd deafening, you're too slow, you're too slow, even slower mate, and you, and you, I'm going to make it, I'm going to make, edge of the pitch, the exit, I'm going to make it, you're doing it Al, you're fucking doing it pal, come on, keep it going, come on, come on, come on, come on.

I spotted Tommy and Becky, faster and faster, never taking my eyes of them, taller and taller. I leapt into the air and reached out for Tommy, our fingers touching, nearly there, then I was slammed to the ground.

I wriggled and elbowed with everything I had to get the bastards off, but couldn't move the weight above me. I edged forward, the weight getting less and less. I looked up and Tommy was swinging like a madman, dropping anyone and everyone. Becky sunk her teeth into the steward on my back and I broke free, over the top of a copper, down the stairs, another set of stairs, landing in front of the exit doors. I ran at the two stewards and they stepped aside.

I tear-arsed down the outside of the cobbles, eye on the Strawberry pub, and hung a right past a burger van as a copper lunged from the side, grabbing at my shoulder. I staggered and fell down the stairs, forward roll and up, in between parked cars, the police one car behind and alongside.

Brian was outside Fluid Bar, but hadn't seen me yet. I took a right along the cars, the coppers now ahead and an arm's length behind, onto a car bonnet, over. Brian saw me and I doubled- backed and bolted straight for him.

I hit the doors at full speed and the fire alarm went off. I ran up the stairs and into the toilet, ripped the mask off and Brian handed me the jeans and t-shirt. I bundled Brian down the stairs and joined the mass surge out of the bar.

The crowd were forcing the police back and Brian and me tunnelled our way along the pub window and took off down the street towards the taxi rank.

I was in the taxi waiting, when the funniest thing I've ever seen came round the corner. Brian, shirt ripped off, pants half down, huge hair frazzed up in a ball and a face of pure panic. He looked like he had just escaped from the local nut house.

I shouted him over and we sped off towards the coast.

23

The atmosphere in the Fiddler's was subdued. The rumours were flying about that the Flash had been caught, others in the know were certain he hadn't. No one knew for sure and everytime the doors opened, the bar breathed in.

Newcastle United legend Bob Moncur, who had been commenting on the match, got the biggest cheer when he said, 'The lad must have escaped, otherwise the police would have released a statement putting an end to all the extra publicity. I for one hope he has because he was so influencial in Newcastle's victory today. Our twelth man.'

Becky came through the doors, sporting a cut below her eye and bruises on her forehead. I rushed over to her and picked her up and carried her into Brian's office. She burst into tears.

I took a look at her face.

'Nasty little cut, that. You need to concentrate on your defence. More duck, less dive.'

She wiped the tears off her cheeks and looked up at me. 'You were unbelievable, Al.'

'So were you.'

'We make a good team, don't we?'

I nodded, then, heart pounding, I blurted out, 'Do you want to get married?'

She shook her head. 'Hardly, I've only just got rid of the last one. Last thing I need is you getting all soppy.'

'Sound by me.'

'What? So you didn't really want to get married?'

'No, no. I'm just saying it's probably for the best that we keep it the way it is.'

'Mmmm, too much relief on your face for my liking.'

We both grinned.

It was after eight o'clock when Tommy came into the bar, elbow proudly out to the side for Lucy to hang onto and to be fair, she was a bit of a looker. She was taller than Tommy, with black, shoulder-length hair, bright makeup, and she was looking around like she was expecting a round of applause. Brian went straight over to Tommy and told him he had the freedom of the Fiddler's for life. Wasting no time, Tommy ordered rum chasers with his first round.

It was nine o'clock when Sam walked in and the place went stir crazy. I honestly feared for his safety and by the time he got behind the bar with me, he looked like he'd been fighting more than Tommy and Becky. He planted a smacker on me and whispered in my ear, 'I never wore it for the Darlington streak,' then jumped up onto the counter and announced that it was a free bar for the rest of the night.

The last thing I remember, much later on, was climbing onto the bar with Sam, both of us bare-chested, arm over each other's shoulders, arm aloft, singing our hearts out.

24

Rumours soon started about Sam being locked up and what people thought they knew, they now didn't.

Film deals, book deals, television interviews, the whole thing went crazier than before and the Fiddler's was swamped with outsiders looking for the Flash.

Sam and I thought about coming out and telling our story, revealing our identities and going on a worldwide tour, girls falling at our feet, but, well, it just wasn't us, was it? And we had Eve and Becky to think about.

That didn't mean we couldn't do with the cash, so we agreed to tell the full story using different names for everyone. There were two provisos, before we got started. Well, three, really. That our identities would never be revealed – like Sam said, how could we do a comeback if they knew it was us?

Secondly, Sam wanted it made clear to the reader that he was packing downstairs and only used the rubber for the first streak. 'That was my *real* member at the Darlington streak. I want that in, word-for-word, or this is a no-go.'

Finally, with me having won that uni competition,

and still having my mother on my back, I wanted to write the story.

So I started, at the beginning, that first day in the Fiddler's...

PaperBooks

This book has been published by vibrant publishing company Paperbooks. If you enjoyed reading it then you can help make it a major hit. Just follow these three easy steps:

1. Recommend it
Pass it onto a friend to spread word-of-mouth or, if now you've got your hands on this copy you don't want to let it go, just tell your friend to buy their own or maybe get it for them as a gift. Copies are available with special deals and discounts from our own website and from all good bookshops and online outlets.

2. Review it
It's never been easier to write an online review of a book you love and can be done on Amazon, Waterstones.com, WHSmith.co.uk and many more. You could also talk about it or link to it on your own blog or social networking site.

3. Read another of our great titles
We've got a wide range of diverse modern fiction and it's all waiting to be read by fresh-thinking readers like you! Come to us direct at www.legendpress.co.uk to take advantage of our superb discounts. (Plus, if you email info@legend-paperbooks.co.uk just after placing your order and quote 'WORD OF MOUTH', we will send another book with your order absolutely free!)

Thank you for being part of our word of mouth campaign.

info@legend-paperbooks.co.uk
www.paperbooks.co.uk